BREATH OF MAGIK

BY

W. SHANE WILSON

A FANTASY NOVEL

DRAGON & FIRE TALE

Distributed through LULU.com

First printing:
Book Printed in America (via digital printer)

ISBN: 978-0-578-00634-5

MY BOOK COLLECTION:

VAMPIRE HERO SERIES;
    BLOOD BY DAY
    SHADOW'S REVENGE
    SHADOW GUARD

GUARDIAN SERIES:
    ENTER THE GUARDIANS: KYL
    LOST ON GROT

THE ASHAN CHRONICALS:
    BLACK WINGS

THE ELEMENTAL KIDS SERIES:
    WORLD OF ICE
    WAR FOR ICE

THE DRAGON AND FIRE SERIES
    BREATH OF MAGIK

RYAN THE WILDFIRE/ ALBERT YETI:
    RYAN OF THE WILDFIRE

ADULT VAMPIRE SERIES:
    VAMPIRE WARS: BEGINNING
    ONE DARK NIGHT

THE LORDS OF ORDER SERIES:
    DESTINY'S KEY

    LITTLE MONSTERS (kids)
    THE SPRITES TALE
    GAVIN THE GNOME

A VILLAIN'S STORY

COWARD: TAD'S TALE

AN ASSASSIN'S TALE

For My Heroic Trio

THIS BOOK IS DEDICATED TO ALL THOSE PEOPLE WHO WANT A GOOD TALES, INSANE ODDS, INCREDIBLE EPIC AND SOME GOOD OLD FASHION ACTION.

To all the magic users, warriors, and sidekicks, this one is for you.

TO MY FRIENDS WHO PUSHED ME TO WRITE MORE BOOKS AND SHARE MY TALES WITH THE WORLD...THANKS

DRAGON & FIRE TALE

DRAGON & FIRE TALE

In a time where nobody gives a shit about their neighbor anymore, a man of uncommon wonder can be found. Shaun Lee Ash was not a big man nor was he the dashing hero type. Good looking with cheer in his heart yes but, by most standards just a regular dude.

This day started like so many more days, up at 6AM to work out, then shower. He took a moment or two to pinch his hot stuff wife's tight ass, okay, maybe more than a moment. He is totally in love with her, and always will be. Ayla is her majesty's name, the queen of his castle. No breakfast, just off to work. That is the last normal morning they will ever have, ever.

Okay, so are you interested yet, well you should be! Shaun went to work, parked in the far and away spot he likes to use, so some Mo-fo does not scrape his truck. He dutifully walked into the building and set his bum to work. All day he had a tickle in his mind. It was on the fingertips of his mind, but no matter how hard he tried, it would not focus for him. So like all wise-asses, he blew it off for tossing a bomb at a lack-whit passing by.

An explosion shook the whole damn building. Shaun as well as most of the people in the building ran outside to see what the hell happened. There was a blinding rainbow exploding from the ground in the field next to the humdrum workhouse that Shaun had enjoyed for more than a decade.

Shaun stood there oblivious to all of the BS theories of the rabble. Transfixed by what he saw, not understanding why nobody else seemed to get it. This was Magik...

DRAGON & FIRE TALE

CHAPTER ONE: AWE.

The crowd milled around. The police and fire dept came to inspect the rainbow. Let me be specific here: there is no rain or moisture of any kind, just a huge ass, Oh My GOD rainbow. Shaun stood there shaking his head and saying to himself "Don't they see it, come on it is right F-ing there man". However, nobody saw anything but the pretty light. A very plucky policeman decided to look into the rift in the ground where all of this color was coming from. A mistake! Once his head was over the rift, it was engulfed. His blood-chilling scream caused a few people to piss on themselves in surprise. The cop yanked and cried, but his head would not come free. Blood was now coming from his ears. The Firemen (brave fools, no just brave) eased forward and tried to rescue the officer. It was worthless.

One very dedicated soul decided that he was going to help that copper no matter what. He unfortunately got caught as well in the rainbow trap, only his arm was literally disintegrating. He screamed and was still working hard to rescue the cop, but to no avail.

Suddenly a man of medium size and light build blew by the police line and ran head long into both the fireman and police officer knocking both out of the rainbow. The crowd gasped in one voice at the price the single man had paid to rescue the other two. He hung not partly in the rainbow, hell no; his enter body was trapped full in the lights and stay suspended above the ground about six feet.

Stillness swept the scene; the only sounds came from the cop and Fire-fighter lying in the grass moaning from their terrible injuries. Yet, the 3rd fella was not apparently in pain or distress. In-fact, he looked as if he was experiencing pure joy. The crowd

11

was torn between the injured and the man floating in a supernatural, unexplainable rainbow.

As if he were in a dream, the man in the shifting color cloud looked all dreamy faced at the cop and firemen. He spread his hands out until his arms were fully extended out away from his sides. A sudden burst of light hit the floating man and he screamed so loud windows in near by cars were blown out. Blood dripped from his eyes and ears. Then as it began, so it ended. The man fell to the ground and lay still.

The paramedics rushed to the two men lying in the grass moaning first, primarily because they were still moving and the 3rd guys was not even breathing at the moment. The injuries were so bad to the cops head that the medics did not think he would survive. The fireman would have one good arm left but he would likely live. However, his life as a firefighter was over. Well, I should tell you, that what happened next blew everyone's mind. The supposedly dead fellow, #3, was getting up.

The stunned medics backed away. A policeman pulled his pistol and pointed it at man #3, who did not pay him any heed at all. He simply walked over to the injured cop and said "There is no pain, and you are whole".

The policeman opened his green eyes and looked at the man leaning down over him and smiled. Because, he was indeed whole and pain free once again. Strangely he had felt better than he had in his entire life, ever. The cop looked over at the fireman and nodded at him, the man turn and smiled in a sideways manner, mischievous if you will. He then stood up and floated, yes I said floated, over to where the fireman sat holding his racked up arm.

"Heroes always pay too high a price, not today." He reached out and put a single fingertip on the back of the Fireman's gnarled up hand. In that instant the fireman's arm erupted in a mini rainbow tornado. The bandages flew off and light came from every pore

12

in the arm as it reshaped itself. The crowd took a collective deep breath and waited for the shoe to drop.

   The sheriff walked up to the man who had asked for healing out of the thin air and seen it granted. He stood looking at him for a long time before getting up the nads to speak to him.

"How did you do that, wait how did you come out of this light without a scratch when these other guys near were killed just touching it?" The Sheriff asked.

   The recently restored cop said "If it had not happened to me I would not have believe it myself, but you made me heal by just saying so" he stopped choked up with emotion

"I was dead and the medic knew it, but then I heard your voice and my agony left me. I thought I just died, but you said I was whole and I was. Who are you"?

   A voice rang out from the crowd "Shaun, what happened"? There was a woman pushing through the crowd toward the man. She shoved a cop down and walked on him. She was not in the mood to be messed with. She was a beautiful petite girl, tiny actually. She looked scared as she walked up and wrapped herself around the wonder-man. He held her, put his head on top of hers and nuzzled her. Yep, they knew each other, no doubt about it.

"I saw the news and you were on it" she trembled,

"I got scared and came here to see if you were okay, but I saw you make his wounds go away" pointing to the cop. "How did you do that Shaun", she asked her pretty face turned up to his?

Shaun looked around and then steeled himself to speak what he knew he must say "Magik has return to the world"...

   Now if you were not paying attention, go back read the first line of the book. That is why there is no magic left, because nobody cares about anyone anymore. And LOVE is the greatest magic of all; remember this. Men and entire civilizations have risen and fell hard because of love. Love is powerful in a way most people never understand.

The cop and Ayla just looked at Shaun for a moment, not knowing what to say. Shaun just looked back at them in complete seriousness. The sheriff was about to say something when the restored Firefighter walked up.

"Hey I don't give a damn what he calls what he did, he made my arm good as new" the fireman said.

"Actually better than new, you can no longer be burned. Not just your arm but all of you is fire proof. It is a gift from the magic to you for your valor", Shaun told him, and then smiled.

"You joshin' me man?" the Fireman said. "Your telling me I can't be burned"?

Without any warning Shaun raised his hand and yelled "Phoenix", flames burst from the tips of his finger completely engulfing the fireman. Everyone jumped back in fear and horror as the man became a living flame. The Fireman screamed in fear. All eyes looked at Shaun who had flames dancing in his eyes. Even Shaun's pretty wife was terrified.

"Damn, he's right I don't feel a damn thing, ahahahahahahah, WHEW" shouted the fireman!

"This kicks ass man....Hey, how do I put this out Shaun"?

Shaun looked at the man and said "Concentrate on putting the fire out in your mind, once you do that, the outside flames will die as well. You are truly a fireman now my friend. If you walk into a 4 alarm fire and will the fire to go out in you mind from within the fire itself then they will simply go out".

It took only a moment and the flames flickered then there was a little pop as the flames went out.

The man of fire was now completely flame free with soot on him, but his body was unharmed. The Sheriff told Shaun he needed to come to the station to make a statement. Shaun looked at him, smiled. He turned; and then stepped forward and whispered something to the fireman who's face showed shock for a moment, then he just nodded his head and shook Shaun's hand.

The crowd was still milling around trying to come to terms with the miracles they just witnessed. Some just played it off to a publicity stunt or a movie special effect. Some decided this was an act of GOD, while others thought the work of the devil, still a few came to grips with the fact that magic is real and the world has change in the instant the rainbow appeared on a clear day.

DRAGON & FIRE TALE

CHAPTER 2: DARK THINGS

In the steps of Russia near the Mongolian border dark figures came striding through the rocks and up through the earth where they had waited. Hungered!

No person witnessed the emergence of the dark figures, but nevertheless, they came forth into the world once more.

In the top of a dormant volcano, deep within the magma something stirred, the earth shook with it's movement and the darkness was aware....

Far out under the Dead Sea a great heart pounds as life is restored, his hibernation has been long, so very long. Two pitiless green-black eyes opened. With one mighty exhale T'relth launches himself off the sea floor where he has lain as stone for centuries. A lone fishing boat was to be the only witness to this miracle. If you could call pure evil on the move a miracle. The sea erupted in a cascade of murky dredge. The Great Black evil looked into the eyes of the first man he had seen in more years than he wanted to remember, and smiled. "I let you live mortal to witness my coming", then he wheeled in midair and with a slight movement of his mighty shoulders; he was gone.

In a wilderness paradise in North America untouched by the stain of man, pure joy is felt once more by the fairest of hearts. Mischief is once more a foot in the world. The land once barren is fertile once more. The forest murdered by man or burned by nature sings a song of life and love. The very untamed winds laugh as magic permeates the land, the sky, the world...

I am sure by now you have notice that Magik and magic are both being used to explain the events. Magic is the body or

17

source power that is used when wizardry or sorcery is called upon. Magik is the act of using magic. Magic = noun, Magik = verb, understand. Elves, dwarfs, trolls, fairies all use magic to live daily life. Dragons are different for they are a source of pure magic and as such they cannot be forced to perform or act in any manner they do not choose. Although there are many dragons, and every color in the rainbow there are only two that the rest bend their heads to; T'relth also known as the Black; and the one known simple as the Red. There are many red dragons but none claim to be called the Red; not for fear; although fear would be prudent. No, they do not out of respect and reverence for the oldest of their kind.

All dragons feel this pride except for one, T'relth.

Shaun sat in a glass enclosed room where they ask you all about...well, whatever the cops want to know. Shaun's pretty wife was not allowed in with him. She tossed a shit-fit but Shaun said it was ok.

Shaun also told the police that if they touched, threatened or harassed his wife they would know a whole new definition of pain. Since they are afraid of him and since tiny flames danced in his eyes when he said it, they wisely decided to comply with his none to gentle warning. Nobody came into the interview room to ask Shaun anything for a long time. One arrogant cop told Ayla to go home they were not going to let Shaun leave. No, in-fact they were waiting for the FBI to come and take him away.

"SHAUN, get out of there" she yelled!

"Shut up Bitch; he cant hear you and even if he could he cant get out of there", said the cop. He grabbed Ayla and shoved her hard into the wall.

"OH MY GOD", said the Sheriff who was standing by the one way glass watching Shaun.

The room was nothing but flames. The glass was so hot you could weld with it. The glass and the wall began to rise and fall like a giant's chest. All of a sudden Shaun was standing beside the arrogant cop. Just as the cop reached for his gun, Shaun whispered (PHOENIX) and the gun turned to ashes. Shaun grabbed the cop by the throat with his left hand, hoisted him right off his feet and slammed him right thru the cement wall. Shaun's eyes were twin suns as he looked upon the hapless officer who so carelessly threw away his life. Ayla though terrified, puts her tiny hands on her lovers face.

"Give him a damn good scar to remember his error; but don't kill him" she pleaded with him.

The fire alarm was a klaxon drowning out everything. The hallway filled with police, some of which pulled their guns when they saw Shaun had an officer by the throat, hanging him out the side of the building through a hole. The Sheriff tackled them to the floor. When they saw the sheer horror on his old face they ceased fighting him.

The fire in the interrogation room was out, but not the fire in Shaun's eyes. There was the aroma of cooked meat and the cop suspended at the end of Shaun's left arm was gargling blood. Shaun yanked him in through the wall and tossed him like a Frisbee at the feet of the entire VPD. A fellow officer knelt down and looked at the gagging cop.

The wound on his neck was completely closed, but he has a hand print burned into the flesh of his neck.

"He'll live" Shaun growled. "Now you listen to me you sons a bitches, I came here in peace to answer your questions and you betray my good will by letting that piece of shit man-handle my wife. You do NOT want to make me loose my cool", the heat in the room jump 50 degrees suddenly. " I can turn this whole city block into a puddle of lava with a thought, so believe me when I say you all better leave me be...for good". Shaun took one step forward, flames burst from the walls, floors and ceiling instantly "Understand" Shaun whispered?

Forty heads shook yes at once and a few prayers were heard.

Shaun turn his back and walked over to Ayla, put his arm around her, (PHOENIX) in a brilliant flash of blue flame they were gone. The Vancouver police headquarters was silent as water dripped from everything. The sheriff sat down hard and held his face in his hands.

"He was right, we fucked up. We asked him if we could ask him questions and then tried to imprison him. Worse, that fool" he pointed at the scarred cop "Tried to play bad cop with his beautiful tiny wife, and just about got us all killed. Gentlemen, I am going to go find him and apologize before any permanent damage is done, I want that boy on the side of the law" with that he got up ad walked out of the VPD and got into his car.

CHAPTER THREE: BLIND LUCK

Every wonder why some people are lucky or just plain fortunate. The answer is both simple and incredible complicated. The truth is that is in some small way they are tuned to some form of magic. BTW, there are many forms of magic. Earth magic deals with just that, dirt, rocks and so on. Nature magic deals with plant life, such as the ability to make or help plants or trees grow and flourish. Those are minor gifts. Some people are gifted with elemental power; they are literally a force or the force of nature. Those elements are water, earth, air, fire. All of them give you godlike powers, one of them is more powerful, however than the other three put together and that is fire.

The great amber eyes of the Red open to gaze at the world anew once more. He has lived time uncountable, and he has seen the world born and die to be renewed by the one true GOD, the maker. Yes, the Red knows of man's religions. However, he looks with disdain at us because we are the chosen of the maker and we waste this most precious of gifts. He wonders why GOD has not wiped the blight that is man off the world. The Red, not one to be lost in thought for long, turns his piercing eyes toward the west, where great power simmers in an unthinkable form, a man. The Red is not the only one who has noticed this either.

Brick lumbered through the forest on the edge on the desert, in renewed joy. It had been so many years since he had felt the ground crunch under his mighty feet. Any creature who viewed Brick would be instantly afraid. He is 30 feet tall, 2100 lbs, blue eyed, blond haired, grey indestructible skinned giant. Yet Brick has a gentle spirit unless angered, and that is not easy to do. The view of the dessert was breath taking. The light breeze tussled the grass and low shrubs into a kind of hula dance. Brick closed his great blue eyes and drank it all in.

The call of the land and the magic coming from it permeated

Brick making his grey skin shine like polished marble. Brick was half rock giant and half forest giant so, both earth magic and forest magic called to his spirit. Unknown to Brick, mostly because he was not paying any attention, was the fact he was being watched. Brick wondered out into the dessert letting the fresh baked earth crumble between his bare toes. As the giant ambled out into morning sun, he was carefree in his own world and his watcher headed back deeper into the forest to hunt.

It had been a week since the police station mess and still Shaun was pissed. The police smartly avoided him like their lives depended on it, and of-course it did. Ayla soothed him, and loved his spirit and his body as often as she could. Shaun had a strength and endurance that was new and frightening. Ayla had no intension of telling Shaun how she was scared of him, and desperately loved him at the same time. When Shaun was asleep he talked and often had tiny flames licking at his eyes, lips and fingers. The fire was hot but did not burn anything. It was the power inside of her lover boiling over. Shaun's eyes had a new fire red ring around his pupils. With his already piercing stare, it made him very imposing...sinister really.

Shaun lay sleeping lost in the valley of dreams. His dreams were not dreams at all; they were magical history replaying in his unconscious mind. Shaun saw creatures out of children's nightmares and fondest dreams. They came in all shapes and sizes and he knew deep down they were all real and in the world again. Shaun convulsed in his sleep sharply which scared Ayla who was watching him. Shaun woke with a start and said "I opened the planet to magical creatures good and bad, so I am responsible whatever happens".

"How can you possibly know that" Ayla whispered?

"I can feel the power and magic swirling around, I can sense the creatures, and I wish I couldn't" he retorted. He held out his arm to her and she slipped into it, feeling his warm soft skin against her, she blocked all thoughts of worry and just melted into her

22

man.

The magic rainbow had attracted more than one person. However, there is only one person worth mentioning, he stands in the dark parking lot, alone surveying the scene with inhuman eyes. He is older than the mountains, yet not quite the Sea. To look upon him you would think retire pro athlete in his forties. Magic brims and bubbles around and through him. He scans the darkness silently; the only sound is a soft wind rustling the fallen leaves. With a look of utter disdain his eyes came to rest on the point where Shaun and Ayla sleep joyful in each others embrace.

There was a small yellow flash and a man disappeared. Outside the home of the Ash's, there was a small yellow flash and the amber eyes of a stranger were upon them as they slumbered. Shaun woke up silently and looked at the point on the wall where he felt the disturbance. He reached over and grabbed his blue jeans, slide out of bed and pulled them on. The front door opened to find a shirtless, shoeless Shaun coming forth with fire dancing in his eyes.

"Must have been blind luck that you were able to draw open the riff" said the man on the sidewalk.

Shaun looked at him with more than a bit of hostility.

"What do you want here, I don't know you, or owe you anything, so you must be looking for trouble".

DRAGON & FIRE TALE

CHAPTER 4: DANCE OF THE DRAGON.

Have you ever imagined what it would be like to watch two superheroes fight all out in your presence? Well, it is not as cool as you might think. It is hella dangerous, and stuff gets broken...a lot of stuff.

Light streaked down out of the sky and nailed Shaun to the ground, with screams of raw energy jumping around the neighborhood. The dark man who called it down smiled then turned to walk away satisfied that he had been correct about the blind luck. He stopped dead in his tracks as riotous laughter exploded from the grave made by the lightning's attack. The dark man walked cautiously back to look down into the depths of the hole. Lying at the bottom was not what he thought he would or should have seen. Shaun was on his back, wiping the tears out of his eyes as he laughed his ass off. The middle of his chest to his naval was charred black and still smoldering. And still he laughed. It was not a laughed that said pain; no it said I am amused at your ignorance.

"You got a set on you Jack" Shaun said as he shot out of the hole in a flash of flames, like a volcano erupting "If I was anyone else, I would have been incinerated, but I am not. You see dumb-ass, my element is fire and lightning is a form of fire, so instead of harming me, you just supercharged my battery", Shaun stopped laughing and raised his hand "Here taste some". Lightning ringed by red flame struck the dark man squarely in the chest and launched him into the street where he wreathed in pain. Shaun walked slowly up to him. Flames were tickling over every inch of Shaun's body and the rings in his eyes were spinning like mini turbines. Yep, Shaun was pissed, but not stupid. Anyone able to call lightning out of a clear sky was not to be taken lightly.

A few people were watching out the windows. They could

not believe what they had seen. Lightning struck Shaun Ash their neighbor and he was not only unharmed, but fire came out of him? A dark figure was trying to harm Shaun and that did not make any sense, he was a great guy, kind and helpful, funny. He was not a man you try to kill. Moreover, what kind of weapon shoots lightning? And how did Shaun throw fire like that, he has no weapon, or shirt or shoes for that matter?

The great amber eyes of the Red watch the fire scene with a passing interest. It is not often he has seen power used so foolishly, yet with razor efficiency. Perhaps this man needs watching?

The dark shaking blot in the middle of the street moaned and rose to his feet. He stumbled and nearly toppled. "I misjudged you". So with a sudden move of his left hand and the street ripped apart and rocketed toward Shaun. The dark man watched with an arrogant smile on his face. To his horror Shaun just stood there with a grin on his face.

"Slow learner" Shaun whispered. "PHOENIX!"

The explosion rocked the Sheriff's car 5 blocks from where his computer said the Ash's lived. He managed to get it to the curb without wrecking; but only just. Deep down he knew what had caused the explosion. It was not a bomb or earthquake it was Shaun. The Sheriff put his sedan in gear and kept going even though his entire body was shaking in blind fear. As the police car rounded the corner, what the sheriff witnessed made his already faint heart shudder. I the middle of the street, a car sized pieces of asphalt and concrete were hurdling right at Shaun. To the Sheriff's surprise, he just stood there. Then the Sheriff noticed that the corners of his mouth were turning up into a grin.

There was a massive cloud of dust and debris. Pieces from various homes were torn away. Like I said two powerful beings fighting was very messy.

"Oh my GOD, SHAUN" Ayla yelled into the tempest.

A baseball sized rock hit her in the head and she rag dolled to the ground. She laid so still, not a muscle twitched. Shaun did not see what happened but, something snapped inside of him. And he turned his head in slow motion to see his bride lying on the ground with an ever growing pool of blood haloing around tiny head. In a brilliant flash Shaun disappeared and he was holding Ayla in that instant in his arms, with silent tears raining down his face. He looked up to see the dark man smiling at him.

The silence in the area around Shaun was oppressive. It hung thick like three day old soup at the bottom of a dirty pan. Then it started. The very air began to wave and boil at once. The ground, grass, street had flames suddenly dancing upon them.

The Red was happy to watch until the female was senselessly injured. Her spark was now so very small and about to go out. However, the man's spark, which was a roaring fire before, was now...

"Oh Maker" the Red yelled in his thunder voice as he sprang his fore claws dug into the street in front of Shaun.

If you suddenly seen the prettiest girl in the area killed; and then if you saw flames running around the ground like chicks on the farm; and lastly, you see a real live dragon, well okay, just the front of him in the street before your house...What would you do?

"Calm yourself human" said the Red "You are loosing control of your power".

Shaun did not look so much at him; but through him. He waved a hand at the dragon and a blast of flame erupted like a Trident missile into the side of the monster sending him tumbling end over end through the night sky. Shaun laid Ayla's lifeless body down and waved his hand over her. A gossamer-like veil covered her, and it teamed with energy. He was obviously protecting her from what was to be done. Shaun no longer was a man. He was living flame.

The Dark man far too late realized the tiger he had by the tail, and tried to escape. He turned to run only to be face to face with the blue hot flame that was Shaun. The dark man's face began to cook. His eyes began to boil inside his head. His blood and bodily fluid were turning to vapor. The dark man tried to reach out to the magic and transport himself away. Shaun grabbed his neck. Shaun lean his flaming face right up to what was once an ear and whispered "PHOENIX" and then the dark man was no more.

The stars blinked and then they were gone. Thunder shook the ground and time stopped. Shaun did not notice any of this. There were tears of pure fire cart wheeling down the front of his living flame body.

"Calm yourself man" the Red spoke directly into Shaun's mind.

"Not now monster, I'll kill you later if you like, but I wish to be left alone just now" Shaun whispered back.

"She is not dead, Young one"

Shaun went fully back to human "WHAT"!

"Her spark is low but not gone, reach for it, feed it, and call her back. You have the power, use it to heal instead of kill" the dragon grumbled into Shaun's mind.

The world stopped, time stood still, and love called it's true name, from the lips of it's lover; Ayla. Shaun lifted her to him and he reached out into her soul but he could not find it. He grew angry again. The Red said into his mind, "Look for it where you know if to be...always". In that instant Shaun knew where it was and grabbed it and fed it like a hungry lion. Ayla was the part of him that was good and gentle, his heart and soul. So, he pulled the part of her that was within himself and re-kindled her spark.

"AAAAAAAAAAAAAAHKKKK". Cough. "What happened"?

"A very foolish man thought that the world would be better with out you in it, and he was wrong" Shaun said, through choked tears.

"Your such a big baby, don't cry I am ok", Ayla whispered.

"He killed you" Shaun paused "you were dead". He looked into her eyes and she could see the wild fire within him raging for control, "Now he is dead"!

"No" spoke a booming baritone "He is not. He is actually an immortal elf and a powerful Mage at that".

Both people jumped as they heard the voice. Shaun vaguely remembered a giant red blur prior to incinerating the dark man. Now, that he is afforded a chance to actually look at the Red, he is wise enough to be leery of him. Ayla on the other hand was plainly scared to death, which since she was just returned from there, is an area she has some expertise with.

As seen by the naked eyes the Red looks like this. Fifty feet tall standing on all fours with his head raised; maybe 40,000 lbs, maybe more. Head to tip of tail 50 yards at least. Here is the kicker the Red is covered with ballistic armor plating, not one layer, but three. Each layer can withstand a direct impact from a Blue tornado missile without damage. The talons on all five dragon fingers (yes fingers) were enough to rend a dump truck in half, and were attached to two ultra powerful arms. The rear legs were massive armored versions of powerful tiger rear legs, and were so that the dragon could spring forward or up in an instant. That is nothing when compared to the head of the monster. Huge amber eyes rimmed with red flecks and pupilated with bright green. The mouth on this guy could snatch a killer whale out of the ocean and swallow him whole. Each of his many teeth was a missile waiting to be launch at a prey. The tongue was not forked, but could pass for the red carpet at an event by sure size alone. The top of the dragon's head was lines short horns, as was the jaw line. Very good for head-butting or raking an opponent with.

The unlikely scene was something out of an adventure movie, or a horror picture. Three souls looking at one another try to grasp WTF is going one here. Ayla broke the silence.

"Where did you come from" she said in a shaky voice?

"I have come from a far land, deep within a volcano. I like hot places, it sooths my old bones" answered the dragon.

"Are you an enemy or friend" Ayla said cautiously?

"I should think that remains to be seen" Boomed the dragon.

"You do not want to be my enemy, big guy" grimaced Shaun "they don't have a good life expectancy".

"HAHAHAHAHAH" trumpeted the dragon "You are but a flea on my scales lil one"!

"Riiiiight, the flea that sent you careening out of control air mail" Shaun said tersely?

The Red had a moment of indecision pass over his huge face as he remembered the power the hit him so unexpectedly, and though untrained, and without discipline, it was a force to be acknowledged and respected. He would have to watch this one personally. He had too great a power in him to let Scum like... perhaps T'relth influence. He had pondered the correct plan. Dragons were deep thinkers; usually taking decades to see their plans come to fruition, but they are capable of making snap decisions as well. This was one of those times. Red must get

30

them out of here and secret them somewhere while he further pondered this strange development.

"Humans, you are not safe here, others will be drawn to your considerable power signatures. Therefore, I ask you to let me take you to a safe place where I can at least teach you how to control your gift" Red spoke as soft as he could knowing; just how afraid Ayla was.

DRAGON & FIRE TALE

CHAPTER FIVE: RESPECT WON

In the black hills of Romania T'relth sits pondering the hell he wants to raise. But first he needs to see if he can round up some of his type of magic creature; the ones with a tendency to be evil and cruel of course. But where to look? T'relth stilled himself and reached for the old dragon magic, to be specific the sight beyond sight, the mythic far Seeing Eye to exact. He looked over the entire county, and then the continent, and then the whole of Asia. He kept going until he found Rolf.

You might ask the obvious question who is Rolf? Well there is no easy way to just sum him up, but if you could, THE BIG BAD WOLF would be it. Rolf is a massive powerful werewolf. He is without mercy or quarter. He is a killing machine, not just for food, hell no! He kills as a sport, or as he says, a playful pastime. Rolf is pure evil. T'relth is one of the few who could honestly say Rolf is their friend. Rolf likes the Black as well, because they are of the same twisted mind.

The Black who is watching Rolf in his human disguise court a peasant girl, no doubt to rape and murder at a later time, the Black chuckles.

"Come to me little brother, the Black has risen and waits for your council" T'relth whispered on the wind.

One very confused girl was startled as the boy she was kissing suddenly jumped to his feet as if slapped. His face turned from one of shock to one of pure malevolent joy. He looked down at the girl, who smiled sweetly up at him. Rolf love the girls body until they were both spent lying covered in sweat and bodily fluids. He bent and kissed the girls bare ass. Then he stood and transformed into a full werewolf. The girl did not scream but she was sure of her own death at that moment. Then when it did not come she spoke to Rolf.

"Am I to be spared then my lord wolf" she said sweetly?

"You have been a very fine lover child, I am satisfied with your body this day, and do not seek your life" Rolf rasped out "You may be with my child after this, so I want to let you be for now. Know this, I can find you anywhere now that you gave your body to me, by scent and your mind, so have carry not to betray me to any of my many foes". With that he turned and launched himself into the trees.

The girl lay there for a time after Rolf left her. She was not afraid of Rolf. He had been a gentle teaching lover, with tender kisses. No, she was not afraid of Rolf; if anything she wanted him to come back to her and take her again; and often. She finally rose from the warm ground where they had been together and walked carrying her cloths to the stream where she washed herself properly before returning to her home.

Many miles away another darkling walks among man. Although this one can not hide who he is or what he is. Thurv is a gigantic troll, blue-green in color with black hair and black eyes. He has long finger nails that can peel the roof off a Hummer. His pointed ears and gold hoops are hard to miss. Thurv is a killer and pain is his stock and trade.

The villager hid his family under the floor of his house hoping to save them from the monster coming up the street. He sat in the corner of the kitchen clutching an old revolver in a bleak hope he could save them from the slaughter. His grandfather told him stories of trolls and goblins but until now he did not believe them. His mistake and not the only one. You see trolls can smell and define each smell individually. Therefore, it is impossible to hide from one. Thurv is a very careful hunter; he will only kill enough to put serious fear in the entire community without making them attempt to hunt him down. Thurv loves the taste and smell of fear. It is one could say his stock and trade. As Thurv approached the home of the pistol totting villager he heard a familiar call. The voice of malice; the voice of hate; the voice of his once and only master.

The villager was blind with cold fear, when Thurv reached for his door, He was about to fire a bullet through the door when the troll just stopped and smiled. Then just as he came, he turned and walked off into the forest whistling a happy tune.

The villager sits alone for a long while, utterly too afraid to even look out the window. A sound beside him made him turn his head. The most beautiful woman he had ever seen was standing looking out the window of the kitchen with a fierce look on her perfect face. Point in fact everything about her was perfect, her face, breasts, hair, eyes, ass...everything. Then she looked at him, she knelt down and kissed his cheek.

"Your family was never in danger, I would have killed him if he entered your house" smiled the red haired goddess.

Her teeth were perfect as well but she had sharp fangs of ivory brilliance in the corners of the heart melting smile. Yet the Man was not afraid. She was just too lovely to fear. Foolish man.

Thurv was happier than he had been in quite a long time. He did not have a care in the world. The very notion of seeing T'relth again, and renewing their killing spree was his idea of joy. That was all about to change.

The forest exploded into Thurv, he was knocked flying into a group of boulders, sending cracks up the face of the central one he impacted. Yes, he slammed it home, or more correct, he was slammed home by whatever hit him. Thurv is a troll, he is big and powerfully build, not easy to injure and nigh impossible for most to kill. Yet, here he was on his butt in a pile of rock dazed. He jumped to his feet and snarled. He surveyed the area, but there was nothing there. No movement, no sounds out of the norm, and more important to a troll no smell, thus no attacker near by. Thurv was pissed, but relaxed and continued on toward where his master was to be found. He had his mind and senses aware now though. Thurv might be a bastard and a butcher, but he was also a damn fine warrior, seasoned and well train in warfare. He was not going to get tapped again, at-least not for free. To bad for him he was not as good as his stocker.

The figure hid from Thurv with ease, trolls are strong and mean, and clever, but let their anger and aggression rule them, thus easy to play with; although, Fox was not playing.

The red trees of the forest hid Fox. Who is Fox? She is the Goddess of the wild, well not really. She is a Werefox, Yes, Werefox. Think werewolf only faster smaller and more deadly. Instead of goddess think guardian, or supernatural marshal. Fox was patient, and never rushes her pursuit. Thurv was not going to go down easy and she was no match for his strength. She was however smarter and much faster. Trolls can take quiet a bit of serious damn and still fight at full force, Thurv could take no less than three times that and he would not even slightly waver in battle. He was a real badass. That was the problem. She did not have time to pick his bones.

The terrain turned from pure forest to a semi rocky mixture. Thurv knew in his black heart he was still being hunted and the change in the country side was going to prove it. The Troll started making a bushwhack plan as he went along to trap the one at his back. Birds flew over head and Thurv stopped and sighed, not at the beauty but at the thought of eating it. The bird shied smartly away as the famous black tooth smile of a predator that gleamed once more.

One thing suddenly led to another in fast forward. Thurv hit the ground so hard that a full body print was made. More importantly he had something burning in his eyes and could not see to defend himself. Thurv felt fear creep into his black heart, only to be met by malice and evil. Fear died instantly only to be replaced by insane rage.

(You have finally made an error fool, Thurv said to himself) Out loud he said "So, you finally want to stand and fight, very good. I love to keep up on my killing. I think I will find a way to make yours last a while". When no answer came and there was no movement or smell, Thurv began to wonder what kind of attacker he faced. Patient to be sure, and deftly cleaver.

There was dead silence as the Troll sat up and spit out blood. A moment ago he was wondering if he was once again alone, when he was hit so bloody hard in the chin, he back flipped. He was not alone! Thurv is not like other Trolls, he is special and feared among even his own kind. Thurv can with great effort use a bat-like radar, and he did so now.

"Eeeeeeeeeeerah" he screeched. Then again as he turned his head one way then another. Thurv shot a fist out in what looked like a blind punch, that suddenly shot sideways and struck home on the attacker trying to blind side him again. Thurv was no fool though to be celebrating a single strike, and he seriously doubted that his attacker could be laid low by a single blow. No, this was a professional killer like himself. Thus, he was ready for a counter strike. However, it did not come. Moreover, there was no smell of blood, saliva, sweat... nothing. "Eeeeerak, cough, cough"!

The sudden knife edge blow that exploded into Thurv's Adam's apple was such a surprise that the troll king did not even trying to counter strike even though it was plain where the blow was delivered from. Thurv tried to use his sonar and was turned away with nothing but a sad gurgle. The opponent had partially crushed his throat.

"HAHAHAHA, well done mine enemy, I can't wait to see your face just before I kill you of course", said the troll with genuine mirth in his gravely voice. "You have drawn my blood, crushed my throat and took away my sight, you are a clever warrior, and I will grant you that. Don't you want to gloat a little, after all, not many have ever put me to the ground, and nobody this handily. At the very least let me know your name"?

"Her name is Fox, and if I had not come when I did; then you would be dead my old comrade" said a harsh voice, that Thurv would know anywhere.

The clearing was no more silent than before as Fox looked over the new arrival, then turning to look carefully at the troll.

"Well , what are you waiting for Rolf kill that fox and help me find something to get this shit out of my eyes, so I can look at my enemies dead twisted body", growled the troll.

"I should think not for two very good reasons, number 1, last time I tried to help you in a combat situation, you tried to kill me and told me to never get in your way or fight again. Second, I know Fox, and she is a master Killer, and you can't help me fight her, thus my chances of survival are not as good as I would like. Oh, what to do" said the wolf in man's clothing? The swift as the wind Rolf snatched Thurv off the ground like a rag doll while transforming and ran in full werewolf mode as fast as he could away from Fox.

Water splashed loudly as Thurv dunked his head in the river again and again trying to clear his vision. Rolf just stood with his eyes burning down the country side in hopes he would not see Fox emerge. Thurv having finally regained his sight, but not his honor was in a foul humor and decide to berate Rolf.

"Why did you run away like a cowered, instead of standing and fighting this Fox person, lost your backbone as well as your nerve eh", spat the troll in anger.

Craaaack! The troll was sent hurdling into the river by a swift deadly backhand. If any another troll other than Thurv would have received that blow their head would have been missing from their ugly shoulders. Lucky for Thurv he was nigh indestructible. Yet that blow would leave a lasting impression even on Thurv. Thurv had, in his rage forgotten who it was he was yelling at. Rolf in full werewolf form was nearly as big as Thurv and just as strong as far as he knew. Rolf was just plain as day faster though.

"**WATCH YOUR MOUTH, TROLL**" a deadly howling voice growled. "I saved your worthless hide; I can't fight Fox and protect you at the same time. Although, there is no love lost between us, you are still my brother in blood and mayhem and I would not see you slaughtered by my old enemy. Make NO mistake she would have killed you, and if I had stood and fought on her term, my life had a 60% chance being lost. Remember this, never fight that BITCH on her term, or you will surely die" Rolf finished and turned back to the landscape to begin searching for Fox.

Thurv crawled out of the ice cold water and sat on a rotting log, mulling over the days events. Then he laughed and dug his nails into the log. "Fox huh, well she is on my list to kill from here on out, but you got to give her, her due. She kicked my arse but good. I say aloud you have my respect Fox and my oath I shall have your blood on my hands before they lay me low" said the troll.

DRAGON & FIRE TALE

CHAPTER SIX: LESSONS TO LEARN

In a mountain cave somewhere secret and safe Shaun is about to get the first of many lesson in magic. Now Shaun was more curious than afraid of the Red. Ayla was still very weary of the great Red wonder. No matter what Shaun thought, she knew that the Dragon was not to be trusted; he had an agenda of his own. Ayla believed that Red just wanted to control Shaun like a pet, crazy power and all. Red watched Ayla with a practiced and measured eye as well, he knew of her mistrust and also the truth of what they both knew. Shaun was going to be controlled, but she was wrong about one thing, Red did not want to do the controlling, he was old, so damn old and comfortable in his power and mantle, he had no yearning for more power and more, he did not want to have a pet. Especially, one that could cook him in anger.

There was so much to think about and learn. Yes he was still angry. That did not stop him from wanting the knowledge that the dragon was going to give him. Yes, a dragon, can you believe that shit, a real dragon. Shaun felt that there was a lot that the Red was holding back from him, and that made him even more curious.

"Why are you helping me, or us? What could you possible get from all of this?", Shaun asked the dragon.

"A simply answer would be that you, Shaun, personally awakened me from my eternal slumber. Somehow, I do not think you would accept this alone. Thus, I will tell you I am not the only dragon out there in the world and not all of them are friendly. I am old and know these things, so I will train you to control your gift and protect your self against the evils in this world. From the moment we woke, the magical creature of myth and legend; YOU have been at war Shaun" Red said as softly as he could into Shaun's mind. Ayla was able to hear it as well, as a simply courtesy. The Red knew even though she was only a human woman she was going to make a dangerous enemy if evoked.

"War what are you talking about, what war", Shaun asked?

"Good verses evil, what else" the Red told him, "Therefore you must learn as fast as you can, and be as proficient as possible in a small amount of time".

"Can't we just hide and stay out of your war, it is not our problem, we didn't ask for this, and we don't want any of it" Ayla said from between tightly clenched teeth?!

"I am afraid not little one, you see your mate is going to be very popular on both sides of the war, until it is settle which side gets him, and his power", the great red dragon said with a tinged of sadness in his grand voice. "It is not my war; it is the war for everything, life, liberty, love, a future. If Shaun declines to help, then the outcome might be slavery for you and him, all of us still living. Imagine a world where you are nothing but a plaything to be rape or kill at another's whim. It will come to pass if we don't stand up for our belief in what is right and just".

"What if I told you I don't believe any of what you're saying, what if you're the evil one how would we know", Ayla said with repressed anger.

The Red looked the tiny woman groping for the right words, but he could see that she was more frightened than angry.

"I would know". Shaun said in a flat tone.

Both Ayla and the Red looked at him for a long time. Shaun was not even looking at them. He at that exact moment had a ball of flame swirling around his hand, between his fingers like a trained mouse.

"I would know because our host has opened his mind to me"
Shaun now looked at them, but the fire kept playing as if it were
alive and free to choose it's own way " now that he has I am able
to link with his mind at will".

The Red's giant eyes went wide in shock and despair, he had not
foreseen this. There are too many secrets, and knowledge Shaun
is not ready for. If he was not extremely careful he might loose
Shaun and the world in a single instant. The Red was about to
say this out loud, when Shaun took Ayla's hand and walked
toward their sleeping area. For now the Red held his peace.

"Baby, can't we just slip away, I mean, do you really know if we
can trust that giant lizard not to kill and eat us", said Ayla with a
hint of malice?

"He is not a lizard; he is in fact a vastly powerful old dragon. If
we had run into trolls or ogres we might have been killed" Shaun
responded gently.

"Are those things really out there, I mean they aren't real are
they" she said with fear and something else?

"Yes".

   Shaun held his little bride to his chest and slowly rocked her
while she listed to the beating of his heart. Silent tears rolled
down his chest as the rain drops of Ayla's eyes fell. Shaun heated
up his body and the tears became a tiny steam cloud without
harming Ayla's delicate body. Shaun picked up his girl and took
her and laid her down on their bed. She protested but he put a
loving hand on her head and she laid back and fell into a
dreamless sleep.

   The dragon was waiting for Shaun when he returned to the
opening of their cavern home. They looked at each other with
silent agreement that Ayla was to be babied and protected at all
costs. Shaun because she was his; and The Red because he

wanted Shaun to be mentally sharp and focused for what was to come. Without Ayla with the program, it would be an up hill fight the enter way.

"We both know I can read your thoughts so, let us not pretend with each other" Shaun said while looking out at the valley, " I might be able to see the knowledge in your mind, but I don't understand any of it. So, there is no danger of me loosing myself in powerful magic".

"You are wiser than I thought a human man could ever be; I ask your pardon for the slight. I will try to not stereotype you further" the Red stated in his gruff gravel voice.

"I will not call you master, nor will I bend a knee to you...ever" Shaun offered.

The Red smiled at Shaun, which would scare a starving dog off a juicy fresh pork chop. Yes, it was not a pretty site to see.

"I expected as much" stated the dragon, "you have great pride within you, and strength".

"It is not pride that makes me say that, but respect, for me and you. If I am going to survive, I cannot think of anyone as my better. Not even you...Argast".

The dragon roared, and the sheer force of his voice flattened Shaun, who was blown right into the cavern wall. The dragon advanced on Shaun who laid still in the darkness. Then he came up short and fast to a stop. Shaun was leaning against the wall in the pitch black, which is not problem for a dragon that can see in the dark. But the Dragon did not like what he saw in that dark. Shaun did not have eyes; he had tiny burning suns where his eyes should have been, and a very serious calm face.

"Think carefully, better be sure" Shaun said.

The dragon backed away and sat down heavily, but never took his eyes from Shaun's. The Red did not know fear, at-least not for the last million or so years. However, an unfamiliar, nearly forgotten tremor ran freely along his mighty spiked back. He did not know whether this was fear or an ample dose of caution. Which ever it was he did not mistake Shaun's meaning. The Red searched for the right thing to explain he reaction, but now was most definitely not the right time to try. He was aware of the power coming from Shaun, and though The Red was not worried about dying, he was able to entertain it looking into the merciless eyes of his would be pupil.

"I take it you were surprised that I knew your true name, the one GOD gave you personally" Shaun said with silky softness?

"Yes, only the All Mighty was ever allowed to call me that, none have ever dared to utter it to me openly. I had thought that all who knew it were long dead. I myself had forgotten it long ago" the dragon said in a shame faced yet proud way.

"If you would rather I can refrain from ever calling you by your given name" Shaun paused as if he had something on his mind and was weighing it. But he must have decided to hold it for now, because he did not speak further.

"It is inexcusable for my behavior as a host and teacher to bellow at you. I ask for your forgiveness. You are not old enough, and my world is unknown to you. I took offense to your use of my true name as an insult, when plainly it was not", the great red dragon put his head on the cavern floor in front of Shaun and closed his eyes.

Shaun understood this to be a gesture of respect and trust. The dragon finally opened his eyes to find Shaun face down with his eyes closed as well. The old dragon felt ashamed, and strangely relieved to find that he had not planted a seed of distrust or discord.

"You owe me no homage, little man, it is not you who has done wrong but I" Argast said.

"I know who you are and I also know in principal what you are to other dragons, their king, leader or something of its like in a draconian" Shaun said "but your metal has not been tested in a great long while, so your authority is likely to be soon".

"Then we shall both practice our art and be ready for whatever may come" Argast said while doing his best ironic grin.

"Well, one things that needs little practice is that roar, really quite outstanding actually" Shaun said stifling a laugh.

The two lonely figures descended into the valley away from the cavern so as not to disturb the sleeping girl. She was way to fragile and small to understand and shoulder the massive burden that Argast knew her mate must hoist. Presently Argast had learned that he was not above new lessons himself, Shaun had re-taught him humility and respect. Shaun learned that Argast was vain and very private about himself, thus Shaun might know a thing but unless the dragon opened the subject himself, it was better to not test him further. All in all the learning had truly begun.

CHAPTER 7: DREAMS OF A BLACK DEATH.

The black mist descended on the figure that ran in a blind terror from an unseen attacker. There was clicking like claws running over rocks or a marble floor. The area in the black mist was a maze with no end, the pursued cried and kept moving just in the small case there was a way out.

"There will be no escape for you, my tasty little thing. I WILL take my time with you, enjoy you again and again, until you finally expire or beg for death" said a rough ethereal voice, from no certain direction.

"I won't let you get me, you can't see in the shit any better than I can" replied a trembling voice.

"I am this shit actually, so I know every move you make, every shiver you shake, I will not release you, you are already mine to play with", the voice explained.

"AAAAAAAHHH, leave me alone" the pursued screamed.

Ayla tossed and turned in her sleep, she had screamed out for Shaun many times, but he was away in the valley learning to control his power. Her linen shirt and underwear were dripping wet with sweat as was her raven black hair. A quite dark figure watched her with a hungered zeal born both of lust and curiosity. He is a silent killer. He was sent here to do some killing. She was not his target. The man was. There was no mention of the Red though and that was not the worst of it. The man backed the greatest dragon known off with no more than a hard look. No, he was in over his head. From the shadows he had watched it all. When the Dragon and man had left, he himself was going to bail out when he saw this goddess laying unprotected half naked for the taking. Right there and then he decide she would be his compensation for the worthless trip. There would be no gold for the man's head if it was still on his shoulders.

Malfeezanz was a goblin king, master assassin, and thief. He was a mere 4 feet tall, but carried 200lbs of solid muscle. He was easy to identify; having one red eye and one blue one. Goblins with red eyes are usually very blood thirsty and brutal. Blue eyed Goblins are usually very intelligent, and cunning. Also goblins come in two colors, green and grey. Green tends to be smaller and more evil, grey larger and more brutish. With Mal, he was both, but tended to be more calm and quiet. That made him the best assassin for the money. And he never missed. He always killed the target. Other Goblins were afraid of him. His skill with darts, blades and poisons were the best of the best. Many attempts on his life had been made all of the attackers died miserably. Pity is for the weak, Mal is not weak in anyway.

The girl so lovely in her sleep enchanted the Goblin, he simply must have her. No, he does not want to eat her. He wants to bed her, repeatedly. His lust had never attacked his senses with such a vengeance before. He was formulating a plan of how to get the girl out and away without the dragon and the man coming for him. He was more than a match for a puny human but not for the heavily armored dragon; and not this dragon in particular.

Mal called for his person guard that traveled on jobs with him. They are loyal, deadly and completely without an ounce of mercy. Mal told them to go distract the dragon and the man, and lead them away from the cavern while he takes the girl and flees.

In the valley Argast taught Shaun that even though he could control fire; that would not be enough. He must live to command earth, air and water as well. Shaun was making balls out of water taken from a stream and making them dance and take shapes.

One single dart hissed and impaled Shaun's neck. Shaun fell toward the dragon. Argast turned and roared. The unseen attackers spit several dart directly at the dragons eyes. They struck as they were intended to. However, they fell or bounced harmlessly right off. Dragons are armored completely, even their eyes. Let that be remembered if you ever must fight a dragon.

The goblins were not stupid or crazy, with a dragon in the mix this was a no winner of a job. Their job was to only to keep the man and the dragon busy. They knew that a full on fight would cost them all their lives. Goblins are greedy and self absorbed, they are not creatures that would toss away their life foolishly; the kings orders or not.

"Shaun are you alive" Argast spat out the words in haste?

Shaun laid there on the ground shivering. Argast wrapped his armor plated tail around Shaun like a castle made of dragon, so that no more harm could come to Shaun as he lay helpless on the ground.

Little did the red dragon know that Shaun was exploring the poison in his body? He was not incapacitated at all; he was learning how to counter the poison for later. Shaun did not believe he was in any real danger, so he was not in a hurry to fight back, beside he had Argast to protect him. He could feel the dragons concern, and perhaps horror at the prospect of Shaun expiring. If it were not bad form he would continue to play on the Red's fears for his own amusement. Enough thought Shaun, time to earn some respect; so the wiry human jumped to his feet and leaped over the dragon's tail; startling Argast.

The dragon turned his massive head back toward the attackers and spit fire into the trees where the goblins were hiding, however they are extremely fast and resistant to minor to medium damage. Shaun saw the faint signs of movement in the brushes; when seven darts hit him square in the chest. Then all hell broke loose. Two goblins jump Shaun and knocked him to the ground. Shaun saw a flash of metal and felt a sharp pain in his leg.

Argast's tail was capped by a massive double bladed spade. Shaun saw it whistling toward the attackers and him about knee height. It was traveling in a splashed blur of deep crimson; at the eleventh hour (the last instant) Shaun lifted his bleeding leg. Argast's spade took the head off the goblin. Shaun bucked the other one off easily, because he was no longer playing. No he was now pissed; and being stabbed in the leg tended to make him cranky.

"Clever move, good timing human to take my companion using the dragon's tail blade" said the circling goblin.

Argast was slashing the forest down with his tail and fore-claws. The goblins were running and dodging as if their lives counted on it, and of course it certainly did. Argast, unlike Shaun was not angry; he was very calm and went about his task in a Spartan way, leaving nothing to chance. The goblins did not notice right away that he was driving them to a center point, one with almost no means of escape.

"Your luck wont save you, neither will the dragon, it is far to busy chasing shadows" the goblin laughed.

Shaun bent down and picked up the curved bladed sword of the dead goblin, he tried it by test swinging it back and forth. Then he turned it over in his hand, ran his other hand up the blade, which produced blood. Shaun smiled, so did the goblin.

"You do know that our blades are coated in a special poison" the smiling goblin hissed?

"Yes".

Argast had four goblins cornered against a sheer bluff that was too high to climb and avoid his fire breath. The goblins were not known for fear but they knew they were screwed as the saying goes.

"Speak, why have you come" boomed Argast's voice, "who sent you here to attack us"?

"We die if we talk, we die is we don't, so we don't tell ya nothing lizard" spat one of the goblins!

A single flame shot from Argast's right nostril, it landed squarely in the speaker's chest. The goblin was instantly engulfed in the rich red flames of the red dragon clan's king. The other three goblins jumped away trying not to be caught up in the tempest.

"Next"?

"We still wont speak, and nothing you do will change that", spoke a one eyed goblin.

Argast's tail hit the goblin in the forehead and spit him right down the middle. Right ball right, left ball left if you follow.

"Down to two gentlemen" Argast grinned at them.

"If we speak the king…"

    The dragon shot straight up into the air like a series nine hurricane. The Red's amber eyes worked like a telescope instantly, another dragon trait; a tidbit worth remembering. Argast nearly fell out of the sky.

Shaun and the goblin were locked in mortal combat, slashing, hacking and parrying, attack, and counter attack. The goblin had battle experience and skills. Shaun had the reach and martial arts skills, so it was a well played match of warriors both thinking fast and using the land as a weapon against the other.

"Shaun it is all a trick to distract us from Ayla" Argast bellowed from above.

"WHAT"!

Shaun looked up, that was all the opening that the goblin needed. He buried his sword up to the hilt in Shaun's chest. Blood sprayed out Shaun's mouth.

Argast roar flames into the heaven for such a stupid mistake as making Shaun look away form his fight.

"Foolish human, you have lost your life" said the goblin "still you fought very well, I shall take your head and put it in a place of honor".

The goblin pulled his sword out and grabbed a grubby hand full of Shaun's hair raised his sword to strike Shaun's head from his body. The goblin stopped because he found he was staring into the face of death. Shaun was not dead, his eyes burned and licked with white flames. The flames ran down Shaun's body and dove into his chest wound and the one on his leg. The wounds closed up and the blood turned to a red-brown mist.

"Sorry I can't play anymore. Oh by the way you fight very well" Shaun said as he turned away.

The goblin did not follow him; he stood there routed to the spot. Never in his life, all the battles, and all the wars had he ever been afraid. He was now mortally afraid, and because of it, his body betrayed him, He could not move.

Mal had Ayla trussed up like a Christmas goose; she was drugged but was still grappling for conscientiousness. She wiggled but that was all, she could not get free. She finally opened her eyes and realized what was happening; and what had her. She was a prisoner of a monster. All her girlie girl ways went out the window, forgotten.

"PUT ME DOWN YOU UGLY SON OF A BITCH" she screamed in his over sized ear!

Mal did not think she would be any problem or threat for that matter. So he cursed himself for having her mouth so close to his hypersensitive ears. Mal promptly dropped Ayla on her tiny butt. He shook his head trying to make the pain and ringing stop. Ayla was struggling as hard as she had ever done. She understood her only chance was to get free. Shaun might be dead already, or off with the dragon practicing so he would not disturb me. She chuckled to herself (I think I am about as disturbed as I can get right now).

"Pretty pretty is a fighter" said Mal.

"I am not yer pretty anything" Ayla growled!

Argast saw the remaining two goblins pull out darts and aim them at Shaun. They spent the last instant of their miserable lives watching a wall of pure flame careening into them. They did not have time to scream, before they were ash. There were only two white shadows burnt into the rocks, where there were goblins the instant before.

   The air was on fire as Shaun called on the inner fire he called Phoenix. Shaun burst into flame over every inch of his body, and shot into the air. Argast just fell in behind him, trying to keep pace with the ever increasing speed of the man of flames.

   Mal saw Shaun burst into flames and had an epiphany. He knew why he had been sent. He was horrible wrong about this one man. He was no match for that, if he did not escape now he would most assuredly perish. He grabbed the girl and set his magic doorway up. He could already feel the heat from the man of flame. Mal stopped and looked at him with a dragon following not lead...not leading. Who is this man?

Once more Mal set his mind to his task. The gateway was set and opened as Shaun hit the ground like a comet. Mal smiled and stepped forward and then tossed the small girl into the air where she exploded instantly.

"NNNNNOOOOOO" screamed Shaun as he fell to his knees with lava tears burning the ground.

The Goblin shrugged, smiled and then stepped into the door and vanished.

CHAPTER 8: THE WAKING WORLD

In his office Dan Lowe Prime minister of Ireland sits and hangs his head, trying to make sense of the reports on his desk. At first he thought he was being punked. But, the sheer weight of all the reports can't be a joke no matter how well done. Dan was once a terrorist and a damn fine one at that. He never killed a woman or a child not even by accident. Dan did not believe in accidents, only preparation. Very precious few knew of his pasts, and they are not the type to tell. If they did talk he knew what was to be done with that. But he does not know how to handle this. Monsters for GOD sake! The army had confirmed that they are really out there and active. So far no Irish citizen had been harmed or attacked.

"Troubles laddie" said a smart ass voice?

The man that Dan looked up at across the desk was the most dangerous person he had ever known. Dan loathed him. Strangely though at present he was just who he needed. He all at once smiled like a cat about to pounce on a mouse. The visitor was a seasoned fighter and he was aware that the temperature in the room just change and was ready to tussle if need be.

"Relax Trevor, I am actually glad to see you mate" Dan said with a genuine smile.

"You will fer-give me if I dona bite, lad" Trevor said.

The red haired demigod in blue jeans and a white linen shirt that was half buttoned smiled at Dan. Trevor made women everywhere he went drop their knickers in hopes of bedding him. He lived a rock star life. Trevor was a good man, mean and ruthless to a foe, and loyal, and loving to his friends. Trevor has no enemies...because he killed all of them with his bare hands.

It is said only a fool would cross Trevor and let him find out. That was because like I said Trevor was not very forgiving.

"I have need of a man of your abilities Trevor" Dan said. He indicated a chair in front of his dark Oak desk.

The room was beautifully decorated. There were fresh flowers and candies put out. Trevor took a few of the mix nuts and waited for Dan to tell him what he was needed for. Although Dan never hid his dislike for Trevor, Trevor himself actually liked Dan. More, he respected Dan for what he could do and for what he had done for Ireland. Dan was a man's man in Trevor's eyes; a worthy opponent.

"You're aware that there have been sightings of monsters and other things in the shire, Glen, and the highlands as well" Dan inquired?

"O'aye"

"I am not sure what to do with this. I mean how do I properly safe guard the people of Eire"? Dan said solemnly.

"Listen ta me, lad, if there er any monsters or nasties out there, why not have the Army put the hurt to em" Trevor suggested?

"If I do that, it is an admission that they are out there and the Ministry acknowledges them. No, I can't do that Trevor without cause un' a panik" Dan said slipping into his country accent "that is where you come in boyo".

"What do you want from me Dan" Said Trevor "No, wrong question Dan, what do ya wan me at do for you lad"?

The two men sat facing each other. Trevor grinding nuts between his pearly white teeth, and Dan just observing Trevor, weighing, measure the man. Dan seemed to be working out a plan before speaking. Trevor had known Dan for a decade and a half. He had watched him patch up walls between enemies as a diplomat and he had first hand witnessed Dan burn men down without pity as an IRA leader and assassin. Dan was a brilliant mind and one tough SOB. Trevor was use to being stared at hard so he took no offense, and felt no hurry in his soul that needed to hear Dan's speech. Yes, it was to be a speech, Trevor could tell by the look on his old friends face. Trevor was sure nobody knew Dan like he did, not even Dan's lovely young bride. A girl that Trevor himself had nixed off his list once Dan had courted her. He wondered if Dan knew. It was of no matter, although the thought amused Trevor as most things did. He wore a smile most of the time.

The door opened and an Army general entered to Dan's irritation, because he did not like to be interrupted and was about to explain his plan to Trevor. The general walked up to the desk and started to say something when he noticed Trevor. The general twisted and grabbed for his pistol, but Dan grabbed his arm with cobra like speed.

"Stop that, he would just kill you" Dan said.

"Nonsense, I had the bloody drop on him" the general rasped at Dan!

"Look again" Dan said "Oh go on Trevor just show him".

"O'aye, Dan, as you wish lad" Trevor said as he opened his left hand revealing a Ruger pistol.

Upon seeing the pistol the general took his hand off his gun and stepped back. He was about to call the guard when Dan stopped him with a clearing of his throat.

"This man has temporary immunity from any legal matter. He is working for the ministry directly" Dan said evenly.

"Mr. Prime Minister, this man is a butcher and a rapist" the general spat at Trevor.

The hand that hit the general was to fast to block even for Dan who saw that it was coming, but could do nothing to stop it. Not that he would have tried. Trevor was a real bad ass, nothing fake about him. Trevor was many things, some good some bad, some very bad. However, Trevor did not have to take what was always freely offered. Moreover, Trevor killed one of his own men because he forced a girl once. Dan may not like Trevor, mostly because of his own wife who had nearly not chosen him over Trevor, but he deeply respected Trevor for his code of honor.

"There we have it, Sonny Jim, a proper slap on yer durty kisser what told the bloody lies about yers truly" Trevor said as he stood over the general like a hungry tiger "Watch yer filthy pie hole lad, or I'll close it up permanent".

The man on the floor saw the delicate position he was in and decide not to press his already poor luck. Trevor reached down and took the pistol out of the general's holster just for good measure. Dan's face was a mask of emotions and none of them was good.

"What is so bloody important that you have to get blood on my floor man" Dan demanded.

"There are now dead Dan, them monsters have killed themselves some Irish" he answered with no further look at Trevor.

"Damn it.

"So this is what you're going to need from me is it" Trevor said while retaking his chair?

"Yes, damn it all Trevor" Dan said.

"Him"? asked the general "what can he do"?

"Oh do shut up man" Dan said as he got up and looked out the window.

"Trevor, there is a Yank they say that understands all of what is going on out here and he is what I want you to do. The man must be found and brought here so he can tell us what we can do to stop life as we knew it from never returning" Dan said looking out the window.

"What if I say no" Trevor asked.

"Oh don't be so stupid, you know you cant wait to leave on the quest Trevor" Dan said finally looking at his friend.

The general was about say something when Dan shot him in the leg, and then gave him a hard look.

"Right sir, I will take my leave then" said the general as he left limping.

    Once the door closed both Dan and Trevor started laughing. They got up and walked over to the liquor cabinet for a send off drink.

"Damn man, you shot him" chuckled Trevor.

"I told him to shut his mouth; I will not be questioned by the likes of that boot licker. You're the only man I know with the resources, know how and old fashion hard ass hard headiness to finish the job, so I need you to be the one to find our man" Dan said as he poured Trevor a drink.

"I want to tell you something before we drink and I dona wan you to shoot me too, until I finish me sentence. It is about Wendy, Dan."

Dan tensed until the muscles in his strong body were standing tight against his shirt.

"Calm yerself lad, I juss wan you ta know, she was already lost in love with ye, when we met. I saw that straight away and because of it, I left her completely be, she is like me baby sis, nothing more. And that is the way I wants it" Trevor said. Then he raised his glass "To Wendy, God save her from ya". Trevor smiled at Dan.

Dan downed his drink and put his hand on Trevor's shoulder. Looked him hard in the eyes then relaxed and smiled.'

"Right you are man" Dan said.

The office door stayed closed for hours as the two men plotted out how they would track down the yank.

At the moment both men were being observed by a wee little man in a green coat and green boots. He sat in the tree outside of Dan's office smoking a tiny pipe. His steely green eyes and coal black mane were uncommon in Ireland where it is normal to have red hair. It was another obvious attribute that would give him away, if he was seen in public. He was a paltry 3.5ft in height. Oh he was not young, and he was not evil. But he was not a sucker to be played with either.

The men in the office were talking about a special man Micky could read their lips. He at his tender age had been a spy many times. He was patient and calm, and oh so clever. Humor worked at times where guile did not, Micky understood this, and therefore he had never been out maneuvered. He was not going to let a few bone headed Dodeans (humans) get what he wanted. Which was namely a chat with the yank first.

When the breeze blew in; Dan did not take any notice because he was deep in thought at the moment and was expressing them to Trevor. Trevor how ever did notice and had his pistol at the ready.

"Oh for the love of Saint Michael, man do pay heed, and never turn your back to a window, You do not strike me as an amateur" Micky said.

"What the bloody hell ore ya su-post at be then" Trevor practically sang.

"Well ya harses arse, what da ya think I aim" Micky asked?

"One of the little people are ya" Dan inquired?

"Aye"

"Good, you can go with Trevor. You no doubt get what is going on with the world right now" Dan said.

"The wide world is awake again Lads, and the spookers and nasties are all about once more. If you want to find yer yank, then best not go to America, he en't thur anymore" Micky explained.

"Where is he then...Say what is your name" Trevor asked?

"I am Sir Patrick Savage Mickalean or Micky for short. And no jokes lads or I will show you the difference in pain between us" Micky addressed them.

"Have Ya any Magic then Mick" Dan asked?

"I have what will be required of me, will that do" Micky said flatly?

"Works for me Mick, Dan what r' ya thinking" Trevor said.

"I want ta know if we can trust em" Dan said?

Micky laughed and lit his pipe. He took a long drag and blew out the smoke which became a shadow wolf and knocked Dan to the floor and bit his shoulder drawing blood. Dan tried to fight but the wolf was only smoke so his hand passed right through it.

"Lad if I wanted ye dead, you would have already met Lucifer by now" Micky said and then smile sweetly. With a wink the wolf evaporated.

"Ok, I guess we are all in it now" Dan said.

"One more thing Dan, there is a war coming and nothing we do can change that fact. Stout hearts and steadfast bravery might be able to save this world, wheer doubt weel surely destroy everything we hold dear" Micky said with sadness in his hard eyes.

Both men just looked at him with no idea what to say or ask for that matter. The Leprechaun would have normally been amused and diddled with their minds, but this was not the time for playing child's games with these children.

The journey into the east started that afternoon. Supplies were outlined and obtained. Trevor took his time deciding what personal gear he wanted; which meant weapons. Trevor would rather pack knives than food. Micky was so impressed by Trevor's collection of bladed weapons that he asked Trevor for one, if only as a loner.

"You know some of these are Elvin blades, nigh impossible to break and always sharp. These here are goblin blades almost as good as Elf steel, poison edge, nar-sty business" Micky told him.

"O Aye, that explains why the Prof' at the university say theys are impossibly old and theer ar-ogin is unknown. I see you favor that mid sized sword, take it Mick if you can use it" Trevor said.

"Aye, I would be pleased to be havin it, I had one of its like once but it was stole by those thieving goblins" Micky told him as he buckled the short sword to his belt.

"Mick, whatda ya know about the monsters out there? I mean are theer banshees in the moors, nightmares in the glens and such" Trevor asked in earnest?

"Laddie, there ur thins out theer that will make yer soul cringe, but the werst of them are them that look human but ur not, keep that is mind young fella.

The country was beautiful. Both of them agreed on that as they rode east into history. They did not know it yet but they would have a roll in saving and balancing our world by simple believing and trusting. Sound corny and simple, but all great men or women are those who believed they could do something more, or new, or better. Then they simply did it as proof of their belief. Will power and character had seen man kind through the ages. Mankind does not have great power or wisdom or even art compared to angels, or elves. But what we do have is will power; even in the face of death man will fight and sacrifice everything for what we believe. That is why God loves and carries us forward because we have faith.

Germany was cold the morning when the boys arrive in Hell, a small burg with a metal statue of ...well the devil, I guess. The people were friendly and helpful with supplies and petrol. The girls as usual took a keen interest in Trevor. Strangely, Micky seemed to be getting some play as well; to his surprise; and Joy as well. Micky was a lonely guy, solitary. He did not choose this life style; it was just that his taste in ladies was either elf or human. Elf ladies were kind but did not see him as a suitable companion, lover sometimes, but no more. Micky had never had a human woman as a lover or even friend so he was enchanted to a point by his new position as a flirted with. Mick was a driven wee man and never lost sight of his destiny or task. Their mission was more important than any girl no matter how very lovely.

There were stories of monsters slaughtering entire villages in Romania, Trolls or werewolves were thought to be the culprit.

Nobody however was alive to bear witness to the details of the attacks. Thus the two adventurers packed up and went to the closest township that was not destroyed to investigate. The trip took them to Bum frickin Egypt so to speak. The mayor of the town looked suspiciously at Micky but did not press the matter because of Trevor who was a strikingly imposing figure. Moreover, Micky looked to be a smaller older version of Trevor, so they were thought to be kin. The fact they looked alike was not the only thing, they also sounded alike.

"Which of ya, keen tell me what happen here" Trevor said?

"Why don't you ask that little abomination, I am sure he could tell you, eh leprechaun" Said a angry villager " my sister's family were in the next town and it was sacked by your friends".

"Wat, Hee wheet a tick boyo, if they dona luk like me-self, then they are nu friends o'mine" Micky said.

"Your lying" yelled the villager as he produced a knife and jumped Micky.

The rest of the town jumped back because they did not expect this. Micky however did. He was ready for the man, and gave him a hefty shot to the shin with his sheathed sword. The man fell flat on his face. Mick pulled the sword and laid the elf blade to his neck. The man messed his pants, he thought he was boned.

"Lissen to me bucko, I en't took a life in a thousand years. I am not luk'n to take yers either, If I knew who butchered yer kin, I would hunt them down and burry this wee toothpick to the hilt in the hearts, no matter the personal cost tu me-self" Micky scolded the man.

You could have heard a pin drop at that point, but, everyone heard the goat fart instead. There was silence for five seconds. Trevor burst into riotous laughter and so did everyone else, except Micky who still had the sword to the man's neck. The man smiled at Micky. He nodded back and withdrew the blade, sheathed it and walked away.

The crowd took the opening for a reason to start drinking a lot, and Trevor who was a famous world class drinker was only to happy to join them. They relaxed and started talking; they told Trevor all about the harvest and then who was sleeping with whom. After a keg or so, they told about the sighting of monsters and the murders 4 miles to the south. Trevor soaked it all up with nary a word. The townies did not notice the moment when Trevor stopped drinking and his steely green eyes began to narrow and take in every morsel they offered; but Micky did and his respect for Trevor continued to grow.

DRAGON & FIRE TALE

CHAPTER 9: BEAUTIFUL MONSTER

Fox watched the village to see if any scum where about to jump the people living there when two raven haired men came down the road in a Land Rover. She watched them park and get out. That was when she realized that there was only one man; the other was a creature of magic. She moved around to spring on him. She thought the human is either enchanted to do the bidding of the creature or he is a dark souled man and there was need to cancel him as well as the creature. She began to move around to a better position in which to spring a trap on them, preferably when they were close together so she could take them unaware. As she was slipping behind a building she witnessed a man attack the creature and he was not killed but simply defeated. Fox stopped and listened to the creature tell him he would hunt the guilty and slay them. Suddenly a goat let a big fart go and the village laughed, so she moved right up to the fence. The small raven hair was gone and the human raven hair was sitting with the people and drinking, but not much. He was faking it, I wonder at his game.

"What do we have here" a razor sharp blade slid silently across her tawny throat "A wee lassie, is it. I nu a hunter wen I sees wun love" Micky said.

"You chose your enemy well monster" Fox growled low and dangerous.

The blade came away from her neck and she went to move but could not. She was stead fast, her body refused her. She was able to blink and turn her head but below her neck nothing. The blade ran over her body slowly. He was inspecting her damn him, the nerve. She was about to scream at the dark haired enemy but he winked at her and she could move freely about. She reached for him and found nothing more than a handful of smoke. A deep chuckle from behind her; made her freeze and then face expertly in a fighting pose.

"Werefox, you are" said Micky.

It was not a question but a statement. Fox could see no reason to reply, but she shook her head slightly in the affirmative. He smiled. Fox analyzed him. His sword was fixed to his right hip, in a quick draw presentation. This was a seasoned warrior, underestimating him would be fatal.

"You are not attacking the village" Fox asked?

"Nay, child. We came for the rubbish wut did the durty deed. We is hee for a reckoning" Micky took a draw on his pipe "Justice has come to these lands".

Fox just looked at him "and the tall human"?

"Trevor has come to find a Yank, one with a dragon. We understand that he was around when the magic in the world came awake agin" Micky explained "I am with him to make sure he don't geet killed by the like a you lassie".

   The scene was an odd one when Fox and Micky walk into the pub side by side. The music stopped and heads turn, not the least was Trevor's. Micky had a serious doubt that any human had ever seen the like of Fox before. Six feet tall, flaming red hair to her hard toned arse. A skimpy leather bra over firm grapefruit sized perfect breasts. Her face was so beautiful that you would forget she was in no way human. Fox was the Goddess of the wild forest, the law, and executioner. She had no eye or thought of love and petty matters of the heart. No, this was a killer and a hunter; Fox was a hero first and a woman a distant last.

"Oh my deer God Micky were did you catch this prize" Trevor said just before he got tagged.

The fist was so lightning fast that a lesser man would not only been had, he would have been dead from the sheer force of the blow. Trevor was a battle honed soldier with reflexes like a panther and the strength to match. Still, he was flattened. He rolled to his feet still smiling with blood dripping from his mouth. He would be feeling that clout for several days at-least, but not right now. Presently all his mind was on this hot deadly woman.

"You are quite fast human" Fox said.

"Your not the first lovely lady to try and take me head off love, and likely not the last" Trevor said still smiling.

"I am not a prize, I belong to no one" Fox said sternly.

"I meant ya nu disrespect darlin, if I knew you would try to kill me o'er a joke I would have held my peace" Trevor offered.

"Fine then the issues is settled, are we clear" Fox inquired with a hard look?

"We are Jake love" Trevor humbly said.

The men of the village lusted after Fox and the women observed her to see what made her seem so desirable, her body and face were enough but she seem to be devoid of charms of any sort. The children walked right up and touched her. One very tiny wee child came toddling up to her and was promptly picked up and nuzzled against Fox's firm peach smooth chest. The babe was asleep in no time and he cooed happily. Fox smiled down at him and it made Trevor's heart skip and beat, even Micky was startled by how much more lovely she became. Radiant is more like it. Trevor could only imagine what it would be like to have her smile at a lover in that way. He or she would be lost in her glow forever, a slave to her glory happily. Fox looked up and at once stopped smiling. Every day the people would remember fondly when a beautiful monster walked into their lives and enriched them.

DRAGON & FIRE TALE

CHAPTER 10: ELF MAGE.

In a dream as old as the earth a mind reflects not for the first time on the events that brought him to this place in time. You can say deep thoughts were a normal habit with this guy. He was not giving the sudden judgments and rashness; he always thought ten possible moves ahead so he was never surprised. But he was surprised wasn't he, and more to the point he had been beaten and injured. He has only now begun to feel fully recovered from the pains and maladies. This vexed him greatly. It did not make sense no matter what angle he inspected the events from. He had in his long life backed dragons down, killed trolls, goblins, giants. In fact he had never been defeated because he was always prepared with a good back up plan. He never faced a foe on their terms; but his own. Of all the un-conscionable things, he had been beaten by a human. Not just beaten, no. He was annihilated. The man was not even a wizard like Sayu of the east, who he had a good deal of respect for because of her great powers.

Orrin was an immortal elf mage. He fancied himself the most powerful magic user alive next to the great two. Even Sayu would not brave his anger or tempt it. So, how could a mere human do what I could not do? He brought back the wild magic, and it obeys him. Orrin was a blond haired, fine featured fellow. He was nearly as lovely as Fox is. Except for his eyes they were the only thing that gave away any hint of his true age. As elves grow old, their bodies stay young. But they develop yellow circles around their pupils inside the eyes, until there is no eye color but yellow. Orrin had only yellow at present.

The elf poured water into a bowl and began to scry for the human. The image was not clear but he saw fire all around. He could not make sense of this. He was not looking for fire, he wanted the man. Orrin said some ancient elf magic words and the picture began to strength. The whole room was suddenly fire; it as filled with the pure fire or inferno. Orrin toss up a magic shield charm just in time to save himself from a few extra months a healing. Elves are impossible to destroy, being immortal.

It is said that the pure flame of the inferno could destroy even elf-born. The pure flame of the inferno is thought to be the first fire God allowed into the world. The divine spark is another name for this. Orrin never thought to be face with it in his life. There is no plan to defend from it, so he was nearly ended. He sat back against the wall, heart pounding, and sweat running down his face. How could this be? He gave the scry a deep thought. No he had spoken the words correctly; he had used them a million times. It must be the wild magic protecting this man. Oh but why????

The study was clean and dry when Orrin entered it. As Orrin had been leaving the lab he made a mindless gesture and all the damage from the fire was gone. Orin knew his power was not diminished in even the most miniscule way all of these years. So here in his study, Orrin intended to find the answer in his vast store of books. If he could not glean the answer with magic he would find it in the written word instead. Being an elf Orrin was never in a hurry. He felt a strange urgency about this matter for some undisclosed reason. Therefore, he set to his task with a vengeance. Orrin could hold a book and know all that was from within in mere moments by touch alone. The magic that did this was of Orrin's own creation, and he was quite proud every time he used it.

There is a great glass ball made of diamond and Safire in the middle of the grand table in the study. No it is not the mythical crystal ball. It is a real one, but there is no crystal involved. It began to glow a blue hue. This did not alert Orrin at once because it was still a soft glow. If it were a full violent blue then he would have to pay attention to his company. The room turned green from the glow the ball emitted.

"Shit" Orin said to himself!

Up in the cleft of the hills where Orrin made his home, walked two unwanted visitors. Orrin was greatly put out; he had better things to do. Never the less, he would see to them. Orrin clapped his hands over his head and disappeared.

Rolf was in the front walking his usual long legged stride which is nothing to Thurv who is physically bigger than Rolf being a troll. However, Thurv was cranky and hungry so he was bitching as usual.

"Aint there anything around here to eat, or anyone" Thurv asked in a sarcastic tone.

"For the last time, NO" Rolf growl as he walked" Idiot"!

"Well, there better be food soon or you going to start looking good Rolfy boy" Thurv said because he liked to make Rolf mad.

"Just try it when you feel you must" Rolf said calmly without breaking stride.

The troll was bummed that the wolf-man would not rise to the bait; because he was more bored than hungry, and all this damnable walking was a drag.

Rolf knew where he was going and Thurv did not so he was stuck following his buddy across the hills and valleys until that reached T'relth. Then there would be loads of food and some death as well. The troll chuckled; Now Rolf turned and looked at him. The troll looked back defiant, but the wolf was looking over his shoulder not at him. Thurv turned to see a pretty boy standing there regarding them. Thurv's hunger return and he lunged to be held by Rolf.

"I am hungry and he is food, get off me Rolf" Thurv said in a deadly voice,

Rolf knew Thurv was not to be messed with when he got like this, and he would turn on Rolf if he were pressed.

"You would not like the results of trying to eat him, my ally" Rolf said letting go of Thurv.

"I offer you my hospitality gentlemen" said Orrin "Food and drink to fill even you troll."

Orrin waved his hand and they all emerged in his dining hall. Orrin whispered and the table before them filled to bursting with meats, cheeses and breads. There was mead, wine, water and other nameless drinks. Orrin sat down and took a plate and the food he desire leapt to the plate by his will power alone. Thurv just looked at the elf, unsure of the next move. Rolf decided it for him.

"Eat Thurv, it is not poisoned; and you not doubt already know this." Rolf said as he took a plate and served himself never taking his eyes off of Orrin.

"Excellent fare wizard, I am happy to accept" Thurv said.

The troll surprised both the elf and the werewolf by eating and drinking in a courtier manner. He even made witty banter as he ate the fare provide him. He consumed his food slowly and savored it. He wiped his moth with a napkin and sipped the wine, instead of his usual guzzle. Rolf must have looked stunned by the behavior, because Thurv felt compelled to explain himself.

"I am a king Rolf; I have sat court in many kingdoms. I have had countless dinners and banquets. I have dance with queens and royalty from many of the magi nations. I choose to be brutal and mean because I honestly prefer it to courtly manners. However, this is not my court or the country side thus I show respect to our host" Thurv said in the most even manner Rolf had ever hear come from his mouth. Even more unsettling was the little smile he gave Rolf.

"What brings you this way gentlemen" Orrin asked

"We can't say" Thurv said politely.

"It would be better if we just thanked you for your hospitality and left Sir" Rolf added.

"I am Orrin the elf mage, if I truly wanted the knowledge I would rip it from your minds".

"We are not helpless elf" Rolf said

Thurv looked at his companion, and thought well is not this a lark, he is the rude ungrateful one this time instead of me. Rolf's hair way growing rapidly which meant he intended to fight the elf, Thurv is the bigger and stronger of the two so he just pushed Rolf heavily into his chair and put a flagon of wine in his hair hand, with a hard piercing look.

"We serve a dragon, master elf and we go to do his bidding. We are bound to him, thus we cannot trade on him, and the penalty is death. If you had tried to pry the knowledge from us, you would find the dragons power reflecting your own back at you. That would be no thanks for this fine meal and drink" Thurv plainly laid out "we bid you ado sir, be at peace".

The troll got up and walked out of the room, down the stairs and out the front gate, which opened for him automatically.

"Your friend is a curious one" Orrin said.

"Yes, he is truly full of new surprises" Rolf said looking out the window "goodbye Orrin".

 The Fully turned werewolf bound out the window and to the

ground, he leaped over the wall in a powerful launch and was gone. Thurv was whistling a happy tune when Rolf caught up to him, he looked at the wild anger in the wolf's eyes chuckled and kept on whistling. The journey continued.

CHAPTER 11: FURY

The sky was blotted out by the rage of flame that obscures it. Inside a living sun, screams of vengeance and grief shatter the air. Anything within two miles was struck deaf by the wail from hell. The atmosphere was on fire, the world was lost; Argast who was three quarters dead, would have wept if he could produce tears. In the great red dragon's long life, he had never seen such misery manifested openly. Finally, Argast knew fear. And death walked as a man, and his name was Shaun Lee Ash. A fitting name since that is the fate he has wrought upon the world.

Shaun was not a man anymore he was FIRE, and his soul was burning and he felt none of it. His life was over, she was gone, and he was too damn late to save her. No matter, he would take the planet with him. Ayala's murder could not hide if the world burnt, then he would die by Shaun's fiery hand alone.

The destruction was complete, there was no life for as far as the dragon could see in any direction. The dragon could not believe the power in the tiny shell before him. Even if the Dragon wanted to kill him to save the world he could not Shaun was complete engulfed on the cellular level by the Pure flame of the inferno. Argast had seen it when God had made him from it and all the dragons after him. It was unstoppable by any save the All Mighty himself, yet it pored forth from Shaun. Once more Shaun was commanding it, and it obeyed him. Shaun had clearly lost his mind when his wife died, now he was going to killing everything as punishment for one single crime. Argast had to do something. Therefore, he did it.

Argast slammed his spade tail blade down in front of the man of fire to get his attention.

"You must stop" he cried to Shaun!

" NO".

"You will destroy us all, you MUST STOP" Argast roared!

"NO" Shaun's fire mouth said "You think I lost my nut don't you dragon, well I am... no I was so fucking mad; I would have killed everything. But, I think not, I will not destroy the world, not until my human hands have the goblin scum's beating heart in my hand, then I shall crush the life out of it and him".

The venom in Shaun's voice made the massive dragon recoil. Never, not ever; had he been so glad not to have anyone as an enemy, as he was that Shaun was not his. There was no pity or mercy in Shaun; it was as if all the good died with Ayla. Argast was not sure what he should do now. Shaun decided for him.

"Come to me" Shaun held up his hand and the flame covered sky dove at light speed to Shaun's waiting hand. It took the form of a Phoenix and alighted on Shaun's wrist.

Elsewhere, Rolf and Thurv dove to the ground and covered their heads as the world turned to fire. Miles, away Orrin had shielded his home just prior to the flames burning everything, Still he jumped back in shame faced horror at the inferno.

Further away still Micky grabbed Trevor's leg and Fox's leather underwear and yanked them into the out, as the fire consumed the countryside. The Out is the realm betwixt the natural world and the magic one. It is commonly called limbo, but it is not. From the Out; Micky left a view, a sort of smoky window into the real natural world for Fox and Trevor to see; mostly because they did not know why he had assaulted them. They said nothing. Their grim faces were speech enough.

The black dragon who was far away hunting for a meal in the wild lands, landed and watched with fascinated awe at the sheer force of this display. He thought to himself "I shant want to meet the author of that tempest". Suddenly, as it had come the flames withdrew. Therefore, the dragon took wing and hunted anew.

The scene was a mixed emotion of love and hate. Fire danced for its new and only master with love and malice. The man spoke to it like a father to a naughty child. Shocking, the dragon clearly heard the fire giggle. The Man smiled and the fire once more clearly giggled and blinked out. The Phoenix however did not. It was sitting in its full glory. It was sitting and staring at the dragon with a keen interest. It was likely that the Phoenix related to him as kin, as dragons are creatures of fire as well.

"Be at peace my friend, he doesn't bite" Shaun said.

"I fear him not, only what he represents" Argast growled back, "He is malice and revenge made corporal".

"Yes, I do think you may be right my friend" Shaun said humorlessly.

The dragon watched the man for a long time trying to find a way to help him regain his balance. He felt that if the man was in equilibrium then so would go the world, he was unsure of why he thought this but it seemed to be truth.

The Phoenix hissed like a thousand miles of magma searching for a hole in the earth's crust and finally finding purchase. It jumped into the air and flew at the speed of sound east. Shaun watched it going off into the distance and seemed to be lost in thought. The dragon came forward and looked into Shaun's face. He jerked back startled. Shaun's eyes were the fiery copy of the Phoenix's. Argast knew that Shaun was at that moment seeing through the eyes of his living flame pet.

"Companion" Shaun corrected.

"I forget that you can look freely into my thoughts, as no one else ever has been able to do, I find it very disturbing" Argast explained.

"Try having your wife and heart blown up in front of you, then you will really get disturbed" Shaun whispered in obvious concentration, " I know you are worried that I am lost, mind and soul, but I will be whole once I off the goblin ... and all of his kind".

"Do you think that will make you feel better or bring her back Shaun" the dragon asked?

"No".

The journey east in the direction that the Phoenix went took all that day and some of the next. Shaun was a mask of fury the whole time.

CHAPTER 12: ALONG CAME A BRICK

When the sky had ignited, Brick was afraid not for himself but for nature, for all of his great size Brick was a gentle soul unless forced to be otherwise. The blue-eyed giant decided he was needed where the source of this fire came from. Brick could hear the fury and agony in the fire as it sang. Yes, it sang a song of anger and revenge and love lost and finally of resolution. What was the resolve, to kill the guilty or everything in trying to get them? Brick could not allow the beautiful land to perish; he must go and help the fire find peace before it was too late.

Brick walked to the ocean and called on a leviathan to come carry him across the sea to the dark lands to the east. What is a leviathan? A great sea creature from legend, in this case it was an enormous Tri-horned whales with razor sharp fins. It heeded Bricks summons as they had known each other a great long time. Once Brick had cut and ripped a net off the leviathan and saved its life. From that time until eternity, they would be bonded as friends.

The voyage took no more than a single day after Brick mounted the sea monster. The ocean was almost alive and vivid with love for the creatures that had return to its waves and depths. Brick could feel the joy, and taste the energy in the salty air. Yes, the planet was once more a living loving being. They saw ships and boats along the way, and received both waves and shots fired their way by navy vessels. The rounds bounced harmlessly off the monster and Brick simple slapped away the shells as if they were flies. He did not blame the people because no one had seen his kind in more than a thousand years.

The surf from China's north shore was a glad sight to the strange pair. For the leviathan's part, his true home is deep beneath the waves, and Brick is a land roaming giant. The ocean is beautiful but it is no place for a rock/forest giant to be. Brick disembarked from his old friend and bid him ado. The leviathan sank silently in the black sea. Brick just turned in his usual good-natured way and began to follow his instincts to the source of the boundless fire.

The birds and small animals followed the giant like tiny shadows around his feet. The giant never tread on a single paw or wing. Harpies circled high above screeching at Brick but staying safely out of his range. Giants are notoriously mean and short tempered, thus more often than not everyone and thing avoided giants. Brick was big and ultra powerful, but had a kind heart. However, not so kind he would not crush the life out of the harpies if they came to close.

If china had a monarch, it would be a certain female demigoddess. She was everything a woman should be. She was elegant, lovely, soft spoken, and had a body that men would kill each other to possess. She was an expert lover, versed in every form of pleasure. Okay, enough bell ringing. Sayu is also a dark mage, versed in pain, torture and all the black arts. Next to Orrin, she is likely the most powerful non-dragon magic user in the world, or is she. She believes that not even Orrin dares to challenge her. She also has had no desire to test this belief. As Sayu stretches her lithe body and rises to wash herself, she turns her perfect face and stares at the dead mans body lain out on her bed with a mild interest.

"You were a sweet and playful lover, but you expired to easily little boy, sadly" Sayu whispered and kisses his still neck.

The harpy who was in the window had watched her master all night and who had enjoyed the show, was ready to report what she witnessed to Sayu.

The mage had known all long that she had an audience while she was having sex, she liked to be watched. It gave a feeling of superiority and satisfaction.

"Report Harpy" she ordered.

"There be a giant, the like of which I have never seen before" the harpy shrieked.

As Sayu stepped under her supernatural waterfall and let the water run between her pert breasts she asked "Explain what you mean, different how"?

"He looks different, blue eyes, blond hair, and slate grey skin. He whistles as he walks and small vermin and bird follow him as if they were pets, without fear of him in the slightest. He eats them not" the harpy explained.

"Interesting, I should think a personal look is in order since he or she is in my lands" Sayu practically sang in joy.

"It is a he, we seen him pee" the harpy said sheepishly.

"So, I am not the only one who is interested in the male creatures of our world" Sayu giggled "To think a harpy interested in sex, who would have thought that. I must not be so narrow in my imagination from now on".

   The Asian mage dressed in a sheer gossamer gown of pale blue. In addition, spider web sandals for her tiny feet and then stepped up to her full-length mirror to admire herself, which she did often. She was very beautiful after all, and every imperfection had been magically altered long ago to make her as close to perfect as a woman could be. Sayu is very jealous of other woman, thus her maids as harpies, which are very ugly.

"Take the dead boy and feed him to the trolls, then show me were the giant is" Sayu said without looking.

The harpy looked at the hansom young man and felt her ugly

heart clinch as if in pity. She did not understand why she felt that way. In-spite of her new emotion, she picked up his nude form and tossed him out the window to the troll guards, who ripped him apart and began to consume him.   The harpy again felt an odd pain in her heart. She did not know what to think, she did know however not to ever tell Sayu about it.

The birds let Brick know way before Sayu and the harpies got within miles of him. So he was watching for them with his sharp eyes; that was another thing that set him apart from most giants who tend to have poor vision. Brick often thought if more giants could see, better they would not be so damn mean all the time, and perhaps enjoy the beauty in the world more thoroughly. Brick and his tiny posse trudged along waiting to run into their visitors when they finally show up. When they finally landed right in his path, he was greatly surprised.

"You giant are trespassing on my land" Sayu said.

"This land does not belong to you or any other lovely witch" Brick said sweetly.

"You are quite mistaken my large friend" Sayu giggled "I own all this part of the world".

Brick laughed deep and genuinely "Once perhaps, but that was a thousand years ago, you stand on the plains of China, what was once called Cathay. We have all been resting in the out or earth since then when all the magic was bottled up" He said.

Sayu was visibly shaken by this news. She looked at the Harpies and they only slightly tilted their heads that it was likely true. "Have you seen signs of this my girls"?

"Yes mistress, a great man army is in these lands now, they are of not import we thought because they are puny and no threat" one said.

"I will not give over my domain to some upstart humans" Sayu said darkly.

The mage suddenly noticed that her giant guest was past her and walking west toward where she witness a great tirade of flame a day past, and she was suddenly struck by curiosity.

"Tell me what you know of the great flame a day past" Sayu quipped.

The giant stopped and turned around with break neck speed and snatched Sayu up pinning her arms to her lovely body. She began to struggle but it was all for not. Therefore, she shifted gears so to speak and set her skin to blaze. This was also for nothing because Brick had indestructible skin, so he was completely immune to this tactic.

"You want to know what I know witch about the fire eh" Brick crowed at her?

Sayu relaxed and let her personal little flame go out with a theatrical pop. "Yes, actually I would like to know if it is no inconvenience".

Brick looked into her lovely almond shaped eyes and smiled. "Very well, it is the pure flame of the inferno that you witnessed". Sayu just looked at him dumbly for a moment and then regained her composure.

"How could you possibly know this giant" Sayu asked slyly?

"Brick".

"What does that mean, brick" Sayu asked?

"No, that is my name. Not giant, Brick, as in he is built like a brick shithouse" the giant said smiling.

The tiny woman had to admit that he was indeed that. Yes, all in all a fitting name for this one. Point in-fact this Brick was not regular in any matter she judged giants by. He was quite clever and he had steely blue eyes that were guileless, yet knowing. Not to mention his acute eyes sight and cat like reflexes, no this Brick was not a giant to be trifled with lightly. Sayu had not seen the legendary temper of the giants in Brick, but why temp him if she did not have to. He was still looking at her in a passive way. He knew she was uncertain of him, she knew this as well. However, giant or not he was still a man, and since when could she not conquer a man with her charms. She regarded the giant, he is actually very hansom.

"What do you plan to do with me Brick" she said sweetly and smiled in a very dainty fashion?

"What would you like me to do with you witch" Brick asked plainly "you can not hope to seduce me, or defeat me in combat, your harpies are equally useless. Therefore, I think you should state your intentions little girl".

Sayu's harpies tensed, because if their master said the word they would attack the giant even though he was quite right they were useless against him. However, Sayu did not ask it of them, at this time anyway.

"I wanted to know why you were here, and I learned that. I wanted to know about the sky flames and you told me that as well. You also offered unbidden great information about the age we live in now. I believe that my intention is to explore the lands I once ruled and see if I can regain my domain, bring it to heal if you follow my meaning"?

Brick brought her very close to him face. He gently smelled her, nuzzled her firm breasts with his check, and then simply placed her softly on her tiny sandaled feet. "You smell divine and your skin is elegantly textured, your magic must be very powerful". He turned and began to walk in a free spirited gate to the west once more. They he called over his shoulder, "You are going to need all your powers if you face the fire-man...Sayu of the east", then he chuckled as he crested the next hill into the rising sun light.

DRAGON & FIRE TALE

CHAPTER 13: ONCE AN ANGEL

The mage Sayu stood there pondering the words of the most agreeable giant she had ever met. She was brought out of her reverie by the sounds of machine gun bolts being pulled back and shouting voices in Chinese. She turned and looked at them. It was obviously a platoon of soldiers from the local army. There was a sharp intake of breath as they looked over the mages considerable assets, which were openly displayed through a sheer garment that hid nothing. They might have had the chance to enjoy her physical pleasures and live to tell the story since she was in a sexually giving mood if, they had not decide to force her. Sayu shook her head sadly and blasted them all to hamburger with a snap of her tiny fingers. The harpies just looked at them with no pity for their gross stupidity, except one.

"Could they not have been trained mistress, to show respect, some of them were very able looking" said the harpy who felt a bit of pity.

Sayu looked at her in a very strange way and the harpy got on her knees with her face in the dirt.

"I meant no offense master, I think only of your needs" the harpy whispered with a raspy voice.

"You are not like the others are you" asked Sayu?

"OH; yes master I am just like them" the harpy cried in fear as she knew she was about to meet her end.

"NO, I think not. You are smarter than they; you have some emotions stirring within you I see. I am fascinated honestly by this development. Do you know I created all of you from real girls? Yes, that is correct you were once human girls. All of you were among the most breath taking in beauties on land or sea. I took you and formed you into my servants because I did not want to compete with you, even though I am perfect in every way" Sayu explained. Only the kneeling harpy understood her words, or rather the meaning behind them.

"So I am lost then" the harpy said getting to her feet with a look of resolve?

"I think not" Sayu said with a smile "I am not jealous anymore, but I am lonely child. I think you should be given back that which I took so long ago".

The right hand of the nearly nude demigoddess was glowing a fire orange and so were Sayu's own eyes. "Anawthra bathu geet regoes vantu"! The harpy screamed as her ugly body was engulfed in orange light. The other harpies lurched away in blind fear. Sayu gave them no notice at all. All her vastly nigh omnipotent mind was bent to the task of remaking the girl from out of the ugly harpy prison she had spent a thousand years wearing. Sayu thought to herself that it is easier to destroy than to create, I must think on that. To create is much more a drain on my power than killing.

The harpies closed in on the smoldering nude form lying on the ground in front of their master. The form stirred and made to stand. It was a girl. The harpies attacked her at once; you see that was what they were trained to do. Kill all of Sayu's' revivals. Sayu had forgotten this and was about to intervene. She was not afforded that act of kindness if that is what it was. The nude figure knocked the closest harpy senseless with a vicious backhand. The second was not as lucky. The harpy got seized by her wing and kneed in the ribs that gave way with a bone crunching sound, then the coup de grace, a blow to the back of her neck, which snapped the bone thru the neck scales. The figure dropped the harpy and stepped back, she turn and looked with a snarl at Sayu.

"Why did you let them attack me, if you wanted me dead why not do it yourself Sayu" the figure cried through clenched teeth. All at once, she stood up all the way and spread her snow-white wings in the morning sun. Sayu smile with joy.

The mage approached the girl and ran her hands expertly over the nude body she had created. The girl tensed but a soft look from her former master actually made her relax for this sensual exploration. Sayu looked at every inch of the new body and tasted and kissed certain spots to see the effect it would have. Finally satisfied, she step back while still holding the girls hand.

"Angel, yes that is what you are; I have made you a living angel. You are just a perfect as I am, in everyway, both sexually as a woman, and your mind as well. I have shared some of my power with you as a show of sisterhood" Sayu told her softly while admiring her. A tear ran down Sayu's cheek and the Angel took it off with her finger.

"I am confused" the angel said.

"I did not know the joy of the making. Your creation has caused me to do something I have not in a distant unremembered time done... I learned" Sayu giggled like a tipsy schoolgirl "I do not want a servant; I want a sister and friend. I therefore gave you some of me, and I gave you back your mirror form".

"Mirror form"?

"I am sorry. Once you were very sexy and desirable as a young woman, I stole that from you. However, your original likeness was always in the out, a shadow form of the real you who once was" Sayu explained while caressing the angels hands "I restored you that likeness, except I have granted you a boon. The wings and sorcery. You will not age...ever".

"How do I use what you gave me, and can I still fly safely with these" the angel asked?

"I will teach you everything. I have never known the pleasure of another woman, I am tempted by you child, you are so beautiful even my heart quickens" Sayu gushed out.

"That is how all feel when they see you as well Sayu, when I was ugly I had loved you all the while. I was ashamed of my ugliness and thought that you would shun me if I professed my affection for you" the angel said?

"Mara, that was your name then" Sayu said flatly as if she were ashamed. If so, it was a new first for her. Today was shaping up to be very pleasurable and unexpected. "Let us leave this place Mara and go take a bath together and speak of our future together, you would like to do that wouldn't you"?

"Yes, I am curious to explore new sensation with this body. It feels great but, it is new and I am not use it yet" Mara said. As they turn to go to Sayu's stronghold, Mara turned and looked at the harpies laying in the dirt dead or dying and she raised her left hand, which she noticed had a butterfly mark on it. She Smiled. "Restore sisters, and revert" the harpies convulsed and began to change. Sayu watched in awe as her angel performed the magic she had just done herself to change the other harpies without any training.

Two coughing crying girls sat up and looked at Mara, and then they looked at each other. Mara swept down and hugged them. They were extremely confused and could not come to grips with what had just happened to them. They were not like Mara, they did not have the residual magic's that she did, and neither could they understand more than rudimentarily, what they were now. The once harpy-girls were hugging Mara as if they would die if they let go. Mara for her part was gentle and spoke softly to them. Sayu, who had been their master, was less interested in their welfare as they were simple servants and below her notice. However, she was curious what Mara was going to do with them.

"Sisters, you are whole again. I have restored your humanity, and I have left you an extra gift for your years of servitude" Mara spoke gently to them. "I have granted you a unique gift that will serve you if you are cornered, or feel the need to ingratiate yourselves on man's world".

Both of the young women tried to stand but their legs were so weak still. Therefore, they leaned on Mara for support and got to a standing position and balanced for a short time until they were able to make it on their own. A strange thing happened to them, as the sun shone down on the girls, sheer gossamer wings sprouted from the girls backs along the ridges of the of the scapula. The wings were like giant butterfly wings, saturated with all kinds of brilliant colors. The girls fluttered the wings and left the ground to fly weightlessly around in awe of they feel of them.

Like her angel likeness Mara flashed open her tawny wings and flew up to the other girls and embraced them. She came closed and whispered something to each of them and then returned to Sayu on the ground. The girls turned on a wing and flew off after the giant Brick.

"What did you say to them" Sayu asked Mara?

"It is a secret sister, but a special one, a wondrous one" Mara said "When the time comes I will not have to tell you, you will see for yourself. Mara smiled and took Sayu's hand and began to walk toward the citadel of her new sister, then she thought better of that and took Sayu in her arms, unfolded her wings and leapt into the air and flew them into morning sun.

DRAGON & FIRE TALE

CHAPTER 14: DANGEROUS GAMES

In the dark European forest where a strange bird searches for its prey, that it is unlikely to find, yet it goes forth in its Spartan work ethic. The bird is being watched by the trained eyes of a warrior. Even if the bird of prey knew that he was being observed, it would not care. The search, the hunt was all, there was nothing else only his desire.

"Yon birdie is gon a lead us to the one who burns the sky" Micky said as he pushed Trevor behind a tree. Careful laddie, that wee beerd could flash fry yer hide"!

"Good eye, Mickalean. You have sharp skills, you will not be a detriment to me if I have to move, track and do combat" Fox said with a rare hint of respect.

"Thank'ee missy, I will try to make yee proud when the bloody time comes" Micky said also with a rare moment of unveiled respect. Trevor caught it, so did Fox.

There was movement in the distant woods, all of them knew it, but not even Fox legendary vision could make out what or who was coming. Trevor was the first to break cover and head toward the movement on the horizon. He was tired of slinking around; he was a seasoned soldier and adventurer, not afraid of anything in this world or the next. The human was a born hero, only his over confidence could undo him. Trevor looked at Micky, but did not speak or stop. Fox could tell that the fun and games were over for Trevor, he had changed suddenly, gone was the flip womanizer. In his place was the hard steely eyes of a hunter killer, and the posture of a man to be avoided. He wore danger as a coat, and death as a hat. When Trevor spared Fox a glance she nearly flinched, the transformation as complete and total as if here stood a new man she had not met before. Fox was a demigoddess and saw that she was expected to fall in, so she did, right behind Micky who brandished an elf blade she had not seen him carrying before. In the Little man, she saw something there as well, that was not there a mere moment prior. Power, he was positively radiating it, Not a minute power either, but a deep rumbling power like a volcano about to rip open and punish all below. Fox would have to keep an eye on these two, they would either be life long friends and allies or deadly enemies to be respected and killed swiftly before they put her down. Strange, Fox had never considered humans any threat to her, and certainly never a wee little Leprechaun. She was perhaps wrong, only time will tell. She rather liked them already it would be shame to kill them now.

The Phoenix was well aware that he was being followed, he simply did not care, and they were no threat to him. If you have never been told the history of the Phoenix, then you could not understand how one could never feel fear. A Phoenix is made of pure flame. Well, to be exact they are made from the pure flame of the inferno or the divine spark if you would rather. They are immortal, cannot die, only GOD himself can lay them to rest. However, since it was the All Mighty who created the first Phoenix and sent it to light the world, it is considerably unlikely that will ever happen. Moreover, Phoenix are creatures of light, they know no evil within them; however they will seek it out and combat it of their own accord, completely unbidden. The only known defense for facing a Phoenix is escape. Otherwise, you are a goner. Each Phoenix is capable of procreating asexually, but only if they feel, a real need or are doing so at the bidding of a deserving soul. Many wizards have had claimed to own a Phoenix, none own a Phoenix; it allows your presence, nothing more. It is a very rare soul that can tame and bond with a Phoenix, if you are able; it will burn the world down in your defense. One point that is not clearly known is that a bonded Phoenix can be killed by snuffing out the one it is bonded to; this is thought to be so but has never been attempted. The risk is that if you're wrong, it is annihilation.

The man who is the Phoenix who walks; knows that his companion is being stalked by some very clever hunters. He believes it to be a band of goblins. With a twisted little smile, he almost hopes so, because he needs to let out some of his nervous energy before he explodes. The Phoenix knows this as well and is leading the followers to their certain doom. He feels no remorse or sympathy they did not have to follow him after all, their bad as his man would say.

The silent figures follow at a safe distance but stay close enough to make sure they do not loose the target. Fox is worried, a new emotion for her, about Trevor. He is human after all, what if they have to fight a troll or werewolf, and he would just get himself murdered. Micky on the other hand seemed more than capable even though she did not know why she believed this. Perhaps his fancy elf blade or the raw power dancing around him. He also seemed totally in control, where as Trevor looked edgy and violent at the moment.

If happened so suddenly that even Fox was caught be surprise. The forest erupted in fire and explosions, like something out of an action flick. Micky slapped his hands together and went into the out. Fox's first thought was what Trevor will do. The answer came in the form of a massive tackle to the ground as the tree she was crouching behind imploded. Fox, was a seasoned warrior so she rolled into a dominate position, to do combat, only to realize it was Trevor who knocked her flat. He just pointed to where Fox just was and there was a smoldering crater there now. With a pop, tiny hands reached out of the out and snatched both Fox and Trevor into the out with un-natural strength and swiftness.

(Cough)

"What the bloody hell just happened: Mick ol' bean, nay scratch that what is here" Trevor gargled out as ash came out with

97

each cough?!

"This be the blessed out lad, and you are leekly the ferst man to ever see it" Micky told him, but his face watched Fox. "Out weeth it lassie, whut di-ja see out theer"?

With a stern face Fox turned. "That was not a fire bird that did this, lil' friend, It was something infinitely more powerful" She paused "I thought I saw...well, I would rather not guess. We must return".

"Ya, right and how do we accomplish that wee trick darlin" Trevor said with no hint of humor or malice.

"I have not the power to return you to the material plain, but I can move to and fro as I see the need. Perhaps Micky can place you beyond the battle sight, so you can shoot whoever attacked us" Fox offered.

"Whee nawt, ready lad" Micky said? Trevor just shook his head, "let's do it then laddie".

The forest was burning like hell itself; a sight that would drop the strongest man to his knees in a not so silent prayer. The Phoenix knew that the trackers had jumped space, so he was searching with his lazar keen vision for them to reappear. He was not the one to see them jump back, but he banked so swiftly that the heat seeker projectile harmlessly passed by. It could not hurt him with even a direct hit, but the Phoenix was a bird of prey and war, so no freebies.

There was a brilliant flash and a loud pop, and then there was war; an all out and no quarter war. The trees exploded into kindling between Micky and his target. Millions of sharp pieces of wood hurdled at the foe as sent by Micky's magic. The ravin haired mini attacker saw to his dismay, all of the woods turned to dust with a wave of the foes hand. The man raised his hands, the flame leapt into being, and a perfect firestorm ravaged the land as it sped to where Micky stood.

"By the Maker" said Micky "impressive"! The tiny leprechaun made some complicated hand gestures and the firestorm corkscrewed back to the source, which was his foes. Micky saw a smile play on the lips of the mystery man.

"Nicely done".

"Thank'ee"

"It won't save you...or them" the man said.

The change in the leprechaun was violent and apparent immediately. The man saw it from a distance. The little fellow let go of the damn holding back a power so incredible that the world shivered for a moment. The aura coming off him now was pure as the glow off an angels wings, and it was about to be brought to bear on him.

"Poor choice of words son" Micky vomited out in pure hatred.

Fox had known that her small companion had a vast resource of power buried deep in him, but this was insane. Her respect for him sharply increased, and his net worth was measureless in her eyes now. She could have faced the foes, but securing a victory would have been iffy at best. Yet, Micky was standing him down as an equal, no, a better.

"Defend yer self yee son ova bitch" Micky screamed between locked teeth.

A light so green that it shaded all other light in this hell bent inferno hit the foe stark in the face. The man was ripped from the ground and tossed like a leaf in a tornado. He landed on his chest thirty good yards away. The Phoenix swooped down to attack Micky. The Leprechaun just backslapped it in to already burning trees. Micky was quite presently a miniature juggernaut, angry and unstoppable.

Trevor was watching from a safe distance when Micky went NOVA. The power literally knocked him off his feet. He sat up and admired his friend, in a new and strange light. Who could have imagined this? Movement off to the north caught Trevor's Sniper trained eyes. He could see Fox from where she observed the fray, she did not know that she had a attacker coming up behind her. The noise was just too great. Trevor yelled and waved his arms, it was all for not. Trevor whipped his 300 savage up and drilled a round into the tree next to Fox right eyes, brushing her lashes as he did so. This was what Trevor did better than anyone alive, make impossible shots.

Fox saw Trevor out of the corner of her lovely eyes and in that instant realized that he was not pointing the rifle at her but behind her and he had the trigger blazing. Fifty round slammed home into whatever was crashing through the forest toward her. Fox who never transformed, because she had never had too to beat a opponent, saw what she thought, was her worst-case scenario coming, so she half transformed into a Werefox. She became four times more muscular and her red tawny hair grew lovely and wild all over her. She was still very beautiful but in a more exotic way. Her already inhuman speed tripled. She moved in what seemed like stop action way.

"Hey, down in front" Trevor yelled, because he could see her moving to attack where he was pouring on the lead.

The man got slowly up from the ground and flames were burning in his eyes sockets, he took a step and then a second one as if testing. The heat of a thousand suns burst forth from him. It was all gathered into a vortex in the man's hands and it cannoned at Micky. The leprechaun only smiled a mirthless smile and stopped holding back.

The power coming from these two beings could be clearly seen on Mars. Micky answered the man's fire vortex with one of lightning. They stood facing each other with enough power slamming between them to ignite a new solar system. Such raw power the world had not seen since demigods and titans battle for the world.

"Ye are quite a sight Lad, but I cannaw let you pass me, for the sake of the young ones" Micky announced over the tempest.

"You are fooling with the wrong mother f" The man was about to say when he saw the second most beautiful woman in the world run into view.

"DRAGON, DRAGON, RUN FOR IT" she screamed as she ran toward Micky, and then skidded to a stop transfixed staring at Shaun!

There was a wail of gunfire coming for the woods behind her. She turned sharply, then looked at Shaun, suddenly she made up her mind and fully transformed, something she had never, even once done before. She attacked the dragon with a fury that made Trevor leap away in the hope to save his life; from his all too near by position. The dragon was greater in everyway, power, strength, size and magic, yet the Werefox's onslaught was such that the dragon was forced to retreat a few steps to try to get the situation under control. Fox was in another class, never had the dragon faced a warrior of the quality who was not a fellow dragon. He could actually come to harm here and now.

The scene was such a surprise the Shaun and Micky stopped the earth-shaking brawl to witness. Shaun suddenly remembered he was supposed to facing off himself. However, his foe was as interested in the mortal combat as he was.

"What say ye, we hold our wee testing of each other and see how the girl makes out" Micky said without turning to see if Shaun was in agreement.

"Fine by me" Shaun said although he was sure if he had

attacked the little man, it would have come to naught.

Fox was not one to chat when she intended to kill. This was not about to change presently. She back-flipped over the dragon's spade bladed tail and raked his underbelly at a break neck speed that only a dragon or other supernatural being could follow, not that they could stop her. Fox was as close as she had ever been to becoming an animal, she nearly gave in to the urge to rage. However, she was the best of the best at her craft and she was disciplined in each time detail, even in her self. Mostly, in herself. Yet, she was not fighting so hard for herself, but for the man who could not save himself if the dragon attacked him. This was what gave her power wings, and it was the thing that made her come with it...all of it.

"Jesus, Mary, and Joseph" Trevor gushed as he watched the spectacle, backing away from it simultaneously. He knew in his belly Fox would loose this mighty bout, but he was so proud to call her friend right now. He had been sizing up opponents all of his life and knew that this Dragon was holding back. Once it decided to go on the offense, his friend was dead.

Funny how life imitates life sometimes isn't it? Well, just as Trevor Shaun and Micky were wondering when Fox was going to get hers the dragon stopped moving, eyes narrowed and it launched itself forward at Fox.

"ENOUGH" bellowed the dragon stomping his foot which made the ground for miles quake!

The girl as quick and agile as anything that ever lived was knocked flat. The dragon slammed his foot down where Fox landed. All hell broke loose all at once; the dragon was hit by such a mealy of gunfire that he stopped. A pure human was attacking with a ferocity he had previously thought was reserved for creatures as berserk as werewolves were. He was wrong, this human unloaded a whole cargo of whup ass on him. Bullets were bouncing off the dragons eyes so fast he could not even blink.

There was no damage, but the human's tactics were brave and intelligent at the same time. The dragon could smell the unmistakable odor of pure terror on the human. Argast was about to snatch Trevor up but was knock ass over teakettle suddenly.

"Wait a tick laddie, the human is off limits, bucko" Micky said pulsing with a raw power again.

"Mickalean you little shit, I was not going to hurt him" Argast said.

"Red"?

"Present".

"Oh, snap. Sorry about it lad. I dee naw know it were you after all. You could have declared yourself, ya' know" Micky chuckled sheepishly.

Trevor looked at the massive beast before him and walked right up to where Fox lay on the smashed earth and picked her up in his arms. She was too wiped out to protest his gallant help this once. She had faced a dragon and lived...this was a banner day to be remembered.

"If she dies I will kill you" Trevor seethed at Argast. The dragon was taken back by the force of his declaration, because the human meant every syllable of it.

"Well, boy what is gonna bee" Micky asked kindly to Shaun?

"You are not goblins, and I have no quarrel with you little man" Shaun said flatly "So, I yield the contest to you...this time". Shaun turned as his eyes burst into flames and began to walk again in the direction he was earlier going. The Phoenix landed on the man shoulder and looked back at the leprechaun with an intense curiosity. "Yes, he is very powerful, lucky we stopped before it was too damn late" Shaun whispered into the wind, while still moving away. Micky heard him plainly though, he knew he was meant to. It was a show of respect.

"Right you're er, lad o'fire" Micky answered.

CHAPTER 15: REUNION OF EVIL.

The bloodshot eyes of a killer were enjoying another chance to kill with impunity. His furry partner was letting off a bit of tension as well as they chased down and massacred the town they happened upon.

A dark dot in the open sky grew closer without notice of the two murderers enjoying their chosen vocation; murder, what else? A boy darted out of the barn down the street and was making good time toward the woods behind the village. Thurv let him think he was going to escape just before his dagger buried itself in the boys back and protruded out of his tiny chest. The troll tossed his head back and laughed as he walked over to the dead child's body. He leaned down and pulled his dagger out, licked it clean and then set to eating the boy.

The Wolf ran down a middle-aged woman and took her violently and then whispered into her ear in a gravel voice "Who is afraid of the big bad wolf...YOU ARE", then he bit her throat out. It was mercy even though he would not see it that way. Nonetheless, she was torn to bit on the inside from his reckless brutality.

The dark spot began to take shape, yet nobody saw it coming. Why, because there were two giant killers to battle in the mists of the town that could not wait for sight seeing. Rolf was surprised at how tough the humans were, they fought like devils. Never, in his long life had he ever known man to be brave enough to stand and fight the likes of him. Truly, times were a changing. Still, they must be killed to the man for daring to fight back. He and Thurv would wipe them out to make an example of what would happen to those resisted the return rule of evil in these lands.

A loud slam behind the pair made them turn and flex ready to pounce when from the dust emerged T'relth the Black. He did not look pleased at all to see them. Why were they not attending to his summons: were they not his men at this point?

"Master, welcome" Rolf said with a flourish and he bowed.

"T'relth" said the troll who did not. Thurv was a king and as such, he bent his knee to no one.

This was never lost on the evil black dragon. Thurv could care less, he was nigh un-killable even for a dragon, this dragon.

"Boys, I have waited too long for this day. You have made short work of these lack wits, but me thinks your belly could not be so empty that you would waste time here when we have plans to make" T'relth suggested with a smile.

"We met the guardian of the wild on our way as well as the elf mage Orrin, who I believe is going to be a thorn in our butts Master" Rolf answered.

"Stop licking his boots dog, we have come, have we not. Is that not good enough for your black heart, eh T'relth" Thurv said in an insulting manner to both of his old companions without fear. Thurv has none.

"I suppose your right troll" T'relth relented. "Let's clean up this mess, eat your fill gentlemen, and say goodbye to the waste of time" T'relth said with disgust.

The devastation was complete and total. What was once a thriving little town with shops, a smith, a school and a church was now a burning mass of guts and death. Life would not go on...here. Not anymore, even the scavengers were too afraid to come. Sadly, there was nobody to remember and morn these lost souls.

As the sun began to descend into the night the evil, there was three lone figures moving away back to the northeast. Little did they know they were about to have some company.

DRAGON & FIRE TALE

CHAPTER 16: WORSE THAN DEATH.

In an ancient keep where only the goblins would dwell, their king and master had returned with spoils of wars. However, not all was well, because he returned without the brothers he had left with. Their kin were to say; a bit skeptical of the lame ass explanation they received from Malfeezanz the king. He was, as you say a lying self-serving goblin, which is to say he was not a popular king except when he took them raiding and they made heavy profits. Yes, the king was good at finding easy money, but he would not hesitate to sacrifice you to save himself.

"What say you Mal the king of us all about our lost brothers" grunted a singularly large evil looking goblin?

"They fell bravely while fighting a demon and a dragon" Mal smiled as he told the truth for once.

"Have you no belly for a good fight MAL" shrieked the vicious goblin giant "Have you no spine to let them face that alone, your famous magic not working for you mate"!?

Mal did not like the way this was going, he was being put on his heels and would feel the brutes heels on his back if he did not think fast, and Mal was a fast thinker. Mal smiled and stood up. He walked down from the raised stage where his table and chair sat. Being the king he was above them, so he sat above them as a reminder of who was master and who was not...

"Well said my brainless friend" Mal said in a silky smooth voice.

If he had yelled at them, if he had raged or pulled a weapon, then...then goblins would know what was to be done. KILL. However, he did none of those things. His lack of fire and brimstone, his utter absence of Malice and evil literally frighten them. They just moved out of his way as he walked smiling up to the giant and said two words softly then walked away. When Mal was gone, one of the big goblins cohorts came up and asked "What he say"? The big one looked dumbly at him, and then away. He began to make for the outside door but he stopped at the door and said without turning.

"He said THE RED".

The dungeon is where Mal made his chambers because in a keep the deeper you go the warmer during winter and the cooler during the summer heat. Mal was a thinker. Besides, if they were attacked all the brainless oafs would be killed while he slipped away in the lower levels. He snickered to himself how he had done nothing and defeated a foe he likely could not beat in single combat. Yes, I am a wise one, it is good that I lead these evil trash; or they would end up on a leash for a wizard or that worm-ridden scum the black T'reith. It always made Mal quiver with unrest to think of that one black dragon, in all the world Mal was afraid of very little but, at the top of that short list were a black and a red dragon. Suddenly, Mal realized that he did not want goblins under the boot of anyone but him, damn, he really did care for them in an offbeat messed up way. He laughed and shook off the thought. He was more interested in a new guest to his cozy little home.

The visitor woke up to three naked girls sponge bathing them. A first reaction should have been flight, escape, but it was not. The girls were all young and had once been pretty. They were all now bruised and filthy. A few of them limped as if they were beaten to hard and were forever broken. The girls spoke not a word, but stayed to their task. A soft footfall sounded down the corridor and the girls froze and trembled as if they were one body torn in to many pieces. The sounds grew louder as the booted feet came closer. The nearest girl began to rise to flee, but the other girls grabbed her arms and held her fast. They were more afraid of what would happen to her if she was seen standing; than the girls frightened wrath.

"Don't be a fool girl you will get us all killed, even the new meat won't save us if you anger him. So, stay put or I will kill you myself", said a dirty dark haired girl of good height.

"No, you will not", said the mystery girl sternly!

"You will learn soon enough bitch" said the big girl.

"Don't bet on that, I am leaving here as soon as I figure out how" the mystery girl hissed.

All confrontations were over or were on halt when Mal rounded the corner and looked over the scene.

"Well, what have we here, a misunderstanding perhaps, or are you just the fighting type" Mal asked silkily?

"YOU BASTARD" the mystery girl shrieked and lunged at the goblin catching him squarely in the throat with a leopard strike. Before the goblin could catch his balance or breath, she pulled his dagger and stabbed him like chain lightning three times. Once in the chest, and once in the back and the last in his right thigh. The goblin king went down and black blood began to ooze from his serious wounds.

Standing over Mal was a blood splattered wild-eyed girl. She still had Mal's dagger in her trembling hand. The other girls just stared at her not knowing what to do at this point.

"What the hell are you waiting for" the bloody girls snarled "Do any of you know the way out, well do you:?!

"Yes" said the tall dark haired girl, "It will be death if we are caught".

"It is death if we stay, we are not the only ones to come here" stated the red head who tried to flee earlier.

"Then I say we flee from this place right now before he gets up and calls for help" said the bloody girl.

"What, I thought you killed him" said the dark haired girl, "No matter, let's go".

   The girls crept stealthily up the myriad of staircases that led up and out of the stronghold. Most of the goblins were way to blown from drink and brawls to notice seven skinny girls slithering out the side entrance. When the girls got near the exit, there was one not so drunk goblin guarding the ways out. The bloody girl with the blade was about to slip forward when the big dark haired girl pinned her softly in place, and slipped by her. The goblin was sitting with his back to the hall, looking out into the dusk. The red-gold of the sunset. The other girls watched as the big girl padded softly up to the goblin. She just stood there watching him breath. Suddenly he turned and saw her dirt naked breasts next to his ugly face. It was to be the last thing he would ever see. The dark haired Amazon girl grabbed him and snapped his neck in one ultra swift motion.

"Aptly done girlfriend, now let's get the hell out of here while we can.

Mal moan and spoke the words of healing that an old magic user taught him and he was slowly coming to his senses. How could such a small girl mess him up so fast and so completely? She had effectively killed him, in a blink of an eye. He was not use to girls doing anything but his bidding. Sex, slavery, torture these are the things he usually needed girls for. This one was definitively different, a challenge, a prize to be won. However, for now Mal must heal and then hunt her down and recapture her. Yes, he wanted her as he had never wanted anything before. Soon...

   The girls lead by the new girl in their mists made incredible time thru the countryside. They avoided search parties and
   patrols with ease. Likely; because fear makes you very careful.

However, unknown to them they were being watched and followed by something much worse than a goblin.

DRAGON & FIRE TALE

CHAPTER 17: OUT OF THE PAN INTO THE FIRE.

Ever get the feeling that you are cursed and no matter what you do you hosed? Well, it happens to us all. In this case, Ayla is living it, the curse existence.

"Kala"

"What", said Ayla?

"That is my name, Kala" the Amazon girl said.

She held out a hand and smiled for the first time. Ayla almost gasped, Kala was not just attractive she was breath taking even filthy. Ayla took the offered hand and shook it.

"Let's find some water, a river or well and get this muck off of us" Ayla said.

Kala and the other two girls just followed wordlessly as Ayla searched for an oasis in this land for them to hide and clean up in. They walked for what seemed like hours or even days. Kala was practically carrying the larger of the other girls with Ayla helping the little one along. Kala noted that Ayla though small was a fierce enemy and far stronger than she seemed. She was driven by some unknown force, but she was indeed driven. Nonetheless, her mad endurance was waning. Ayla was on the verge of complete physical collapse. Kala saw a grove of tress ahead and began to steer the other girl toward it because she was the only one with a semi clear mind and vision, and she too was maxed out.

"We rest there sisters" Kala said in a raspy tone.

"Fine with me" said Kamy the second smallest member of the

troop. Only Ayla was smaller, though she acted as if she were a giantess.

"Drop me anywhere Kala, I am dead already" said the last girl in the troop .

Ayla and Kala looked at her intently. Kala put her down under a tree and sure enough, she was bleeding out her insides. Kala started to say this is just your time of the cycle, but Ayla grabbed her arm and pressed gently then shook her tiny head.

"It comes as no surprise the last time the goblin raped me he used tools ...I wont go into it, but my inside were severely damaged" said the dirt plan looking girl.

"A thousand deaths on Malfeezanz" cried Kamy, as tears began to well up in her lovely eyes.

"My name was Kit, well Kitten was what I was always called. The goblin hurt me because I am plan and thus useless for anything but rape and torture. Our new friend fixed him for his many trespasses, so I can go to a better life knowing he will not live to gloat over my broken body" Kit whispered as her life drained slowly away.

"I don't think" Kala started to say but was cut off by Ayla as she clamped down on her arm painfully.

"He will see no more sunrises sister, my word on it. I will make war on all of his kind, and when Shaun tracks them down, there will be no where on the planet they could crawl that he will find and utterly annihilate them...All" Ayla growled with oyster tears running down her delicate features.

Kit died shortly after they put her under the tree. She told them that she was sorry for not telling them she was dying but she did not want to die a prisoner, but a free woman, and she was afraid they would leave her if they knew. Kamy held Kit in her arms and rocked her friend until she slipped away in peace. Then Kala and Ayla buried her under the tree. Ayla carved her name in the tree above the grave and spoke a short prayer.

Three pairs of eyes witnessed what the girls had done. Telepathically they commented on what they wanted to do once the burial was over. It was odd that the females had not noticed they were being watched, especially since they had successfully avoided the goblins thus far. No small feat, considering how thoroughly goblins track. Yet, they did not make a clean getaway, for they were found and once again in danger.

As the three girls were making their way west, they were struck silent and still by what they saw, in the clearing in front of them. Three monsters.

"Well hello there lovely ladies" Rolf said elegantly.

"Hello, yourself" Kala bold said.

Rolf transformed and walked up to the women as a man. He is very hansom. It took the girls breath to see him go from a monster to a pretty boy. Ayla was not to be put off.

"Stand aside, we have no quarrel with you wolf, we only wish to be on our way. We are looking for someone, and you should not want to meet him or his companion" Ayla plainly stated.

"Do tell little miss, who is this man and his dangerous companion that we should fear" said Thurv in lite amusement?

"The man is my mate" Ayla smiled.

"Woo, I am so vexed with fear, I shake. Why do I care for a human, I am Thurv king of the trolls" the giant troll hissed as he laughed deeply?

"You should be fool" said a new voice.

All heads turned to see Mal and a hundred Goblins step from the out into the clearing. All were armed to the teeth and ready to wage war at the whiff of an order. Mal had new freshly healing scars and a wicked look on his ugly face.

"Malfeezanz, what brings you to this conclusion" boomed The Black.

Mal looked at him briefly, then back at Ayla intently. He came to a decision painfully and regarded T'relth fully. The mighty black dragon had waited patiently for Mal to decide. It was a strange sort of respect, that T'relth rarely showed anyone, yet Mal had clearly been shown it to the surprise of Rolf and Thurv.

"I stole her away from her mate" he explained holding up a hand to let him continue "No great thing to steal from a human...usually. Her mate is no mere human, you have seen the sky burn no doubt my lord T'relth. Well, it burns for him, and because of him. He calls forth the fire and it obeys him as does the Phoenix that has bonded to him".

"Bullshit, you lie goblin. Nobody commands fire or a Phoenix. Only dragons have mastered fire as an element" Rolf growled low and dangerous!

"Oh do shut up dog" Thurv grunted "pray continue goblin king, I would know that which I will hunt".

Mal looked at Ayla longingly. It was plain as day she knew he wanted her, not for torture, but for love or lust. It was equally plain that Mal knew he was not to have her again. He was over matched by the dragon alone. The Troll and werewolf were pretty bad, but not unbeatable, the dragon was a no winner.

"I would have you know one thing further, the man travels with a powerful ally" Mal said without looking away from Ayla.

"Who could make you warn the likes of us" Rolf crowed?

"The RED"

"ROOOOOOAAAR"!!!!!

Flames belched out over most of the clearing just above the ground. T'relth was beside himself in anger. Rolf was frightened. Thurv who had fire dancing over his skin stood utterly motionless. The three girls were yanked behind a big stone just as they were about to be turned to ash.

Mal stood moving his hands in a complex pattern. The fire did not touch him or any of the goblins. Thurv saw this and his respect for Mal went up, being able to use magic to dispel dragon's fire; was no small trick.

"Why him, why now, why couldn't he stay asleep so I could trap and kill him" roared T'relth!!!   With a sweep of his wing, the Black put out all the flames. "Come to me child" he said to the girls.

   All three of them got up holding hands and walked toward the great black nightmare. As they approached, Rolf reached out to snatch Kamy. Faster than she had ever moved before Ayla pulled he hidden blade and cut Rolf's throat, ear to ear. He stood there with blood gushing down his chest in complete and utter shock. He had not ever thought that this smallest of harmless women, could injure let along kill him. He suddenly snapped out of his shock, transformed fully, and sprang at Ayla's throat.

   Rolf found himself pin face down in the dirt, with a dragon claw digging into his neck. He was wild with anger and fought, but to no avail, he was trapped completely.

"Let me up T'relth, this is no way to treat your loyal general" growled Rolf.

It was a tense moment for all involved because T'relth was not in the mood to be generous, but then again, Rolf was as loyal as they came. In the end, the dragon lifted his mighty foreleg and the wolfman crawled out. He stood up snapped his neck back and forth popping the vertebrae into place and then his back. The look Kala gave him was a clear warning, life or death she would not allow him to touch Ayla or Kamy. He transformed back to the man he had been.

"Why do you protect them?" Rolf said testily.

His answer came in the form of a backhand from Thurv. Rolf bounced none to soft off the tree some thirty feet away.

"Fool, even I am not brave enough to kill someone that would bring The Red down on my head. Did you not hear the Goblin say as much, a moment ago dog" Thurv had a wild haunted look to him as he spoke. "Toss your own life away, but I do not offer mine so easy".

Totally disregarding the sideshow T'relth tapped his claw on the rocks to get Ayla and Kala's attention. They did not want to face the music but they were not strong enough to disobey T'relth, so they went as they were bid.

"You are a special human on more than one front child. I am evil and merciless children, but for now you have my protection, none may harm you without my say so" T'relth raised his voice the thunder level "Any who try will be met with painful death". He looked down at the three tiny women and studies them. Satisfied, he suddenly transformed into a man.

The shock of the scene took everyone by surprise. The Dragon was no more, now a man of middle years stood looking around. Thurv just smiled and nodded that he approved of this move by the dragon. Who would think to look at a man twice, if he was with a troll and a werewolf? If they did, they would believe him to be their prisoner.

"I did not know you could do that, master" Rolf said.

"You are an idiot" said Mal "Dragons are masters of magic forgotten by the world life times ago, do you think you can know all he is capable of Wolfman"?

Rolf snarled but did not move against Mal, mainly because of the 100 angry goblins standing at his back, spoiling for a fight.

The once dragon, now man waved his hand and the air opened into the out. "Please, after you ladies" he said elegantly. They knew this was no request but a simple command. They obliged willingly. Life is strange, and it has taken a bad turn. Goblins are bad, but they could escape, however, there was no place they could go to rid themselves of a dragon. Moreover, he had Mal and Thurv in his employ so they were trapped. Out of the pan into the fire whispered Ayla to Kala, who did not reply, just set her lovely face into a grim picture and stepped into the nothing of the Out.

DRAGON & FIRE TALE

CHAPTER 18: TO HUNT

In the forest, a motley crew of adventurers, tramp through the wilderness searching for the prize. To Trevor the prize was to be the Yank who understands what is going on, now it is Fox. He wants her, badly. Fox on the other hand hunts but she is not sure what for. The troll Thurv who she wants to kill is long gone and no sign of him remains. The Red seeks to end the threat to this world, there is only two ways of doing this, kill Shaun or help him complete his quest for revenge. The first would be easy if not for the Phoenix who watches Shaun's back night and day, and Shaun himself is a storehouse of incredible power. Yes, The Red must figure this out before it is too late to save our world.

Shaun walked in a study pace east, without stopping for food or water. Further, he seemed not too tire or require substance to keep up his strength. The same was not true of Trevor.

"Ok, damn it all lad, I am hungry and pooped" Trevor blurted out" can't we bloody well rest and eat something, for the love of CHRIST"?

"Yes, laddie buck, I kin feel ya need no rest but we do and so hungry is the RED, he might eat you if you donna feed him soon" Micky said in his singing way.

"Fine" Shaun said stopping. He turned and looked at Trevor "What do you want to eat man"?

"Honestly, meat and bread lad of any kind that is not too old or raw will do, I am no picky fella" Trevor replied.

"PHEONIX" Shaun burst into flames and disappeared. For about 10 minutes, they all thought he simply left them behind. It seemed likely that he would do that. As sudden as left he burst forth from new flames. In his arms, he carried sausages, fresh bread and cheese. He walked over to Trevor and handed the food over. The rest of the party minus The Red gathered around and took some food. It was not old crap either it was fresh and tasty. Trevor smiled at Fox as she bit into the bread and smiled at the wonderful aroma and flavor. She noticed and stopped smiling. Trevor tossed a sausage to the Phoenix, it caught the meat and ate it.

"He thanks you for your kind regard, it is a novelty for him to eat human food. He needs none to live though" Shaun spoke softly for the Phoenix on his shoulder.

"Here mate have some for yerself" Trevor said as he jumped up and took food to Shaun.

Shaun and Trevor ate the meal sitting beside each other. Fox watched them with growing interest. Micky notice and so did the Red.

"Why doesn't the Phoenix fire burn you man" Trevor asked Shaun?

"We are bound to one another, he adopted me you could say" Shaun explained "I have the power over fire of all sorts, he is my safety, I am the trigger. If I were to go too far he could stop me, where as nothing else I know of right now could, not even my friend there" Shaun pointed at The red.

"What do you call that monster" Trevor asked?

The Red growled low and dangerous.

"You may call him Red storm, he is my teacher and friend, or simply Red but NEVER call him monster again or you will not live to know the mistake" Shaun said sternly to Trevor.

"Oh, by the way, you are very brave to stand up to him over the

124

girl, whatever she is". Shaun half smiled then walked over to Micky.

"You're a Leprechaun, if I am not mistaken" Shaun said?

"Aye I am" Micky answered "Why do you ask sonny Jim"?

"Honestly, I was surprised that I couldn't fry you when we faced off. I was sure it be only a moment and I was so wrong. Your like me your hiding a huge power inside of you, why is that. Or are all of your kin this powerful" Shaun asked?

"Weel, it is like this, King Brian is likely the most powerful of all of us, but I am only a wee bit behind himself. As for my kin, all of us Wee people as they say. can pin the tail on yer donkey if you folla me" Micky chuckled.

Shaun smiled at Micky, he had a genuine admiration for the little fella he had to admit. Of all the strange and wonderful creatures he had seen and met, Micky was only second to the Red in pure wonder and power; which is seriously saying something Shaun made a mental note to ask the Red about Micky later.

From the clear blue ocean spray sky the Red burst to the ground as if on cue. He was looking at Shaun and Micky sitting together chatting and felt a sudden despair deep in his massive belly. If they join forces in a common cause then even he might be unable to prevent a catastrophe. Fox noticed his intense stare and directed her own to match his. She observed two of the most powerful beings chatting whimsically together as if they had not nearly burned the world down in battle only hours before...and against one another!

Shaun looked up and caught Fox staring at him. He smiled and she blushed, which is an odd thing for her. She is covered in fine reddish down, like a baby. Her body is taut and fit; so when she blushed, she really glows red. Shaun turned his head and looked straight at Trevor who was looking directly at Fox with a look of longing. "Oh Snap" Shaun thought to himself. What are we really hunting out here? Fox caught Trevor looking at her and she gave him a dirty look. He actually looked hurt. His gaze at Shaun was not friendly now.

"They are so veerly young, they weel be fine my friend of fire" Micky said.

The Red was not so sure, but he kept his counsel to himself. This is getting out of hand, when did I loose control of this one, he thought. They all are so powerful, even the human is a hand full and not to be discounted. No good could come of this the Red believed, it would all no doubt end poorly with loss of life. He hoped it would not come to that but that was just fanciful thinking and he knew it to be thus.

A scream of terror erupted behind The Red as the wood turned into screams of anguish as the fire covered burned to death. The steely-eyed Phoenix was barfing fire into a group of goblins.

Shaun was on his feet in a blur and moved at the speed of flame (think chain lightning) into the fray.

"Stop" Shaun roared at the top of his lungs and raised his hand and all at once, the fire in the woods snapped into his hand. The Phoenix looked at him curiously but made no move to stop Shaun from putting the fire out.

"I want to question them, so don't kill them all" Shaun was incensed. The Phoenix seemed to shrug.

The remaining living goblins made a run for it and boy were they flat tracking out of there. Shaun turned, looked hard at the companions for an instant with the flames of revenge burning once more in his eyes, and then he burst in the forest after the retreating goblins.

"Oh shit, they nearly snuck up on us. We would have been

killed if not for that wee birdy" Trevor said as he locked and loaded his mega assault rifle, "Come on or do ya wish to live forever"!

Trevor blew into the woods at an inhuman pace that Fox found admirable, and she followed him hot on his heels. Before Micky could move Red storm snatched his short butt up and with one powerful stroke they were airborne and in pursuit of their crew.

The raiding goblins were making their way through the trees at a fevers pace, because to slow down meant certain death from the flaming bird or the nutcase bearing down on them. Normally they would not fear a human, but this one commanded the firebird and they saw fire jump into his hand. Goblins do not like fire, especially if it is being directed at them in the form of a weapon. Malfeezanz had sent them to find and eliminate the man if they could. They found him but that damn bird caught them sneaking up for the kill. It was they who were killed, and this was not right on any level. What a pisser. Nonetheless, they would have to set a trap for the man and his puny allies, if they were to escape. Later, they could make up a good story for Mal, to fend off his anger.

Trevor being a terrorist and hunter was careful not to fall into a trap or let the prey circle behind him. He lost sight of Shaun. In his heart, he thought it would be best for him if Shaun were out of the picture; maybe he would get himself killed. No, what they hell is wrong with me he thought, Shaun is not his enemy. If Fox wants him then why shouldn't they be happy, no matter if he was miserable?

The brush was no obstacle to Fox, she bee-bopped and slashed from side to side finding the gaps perfectly. Her mind however, was not on what she was doing and where she was or she would have seen the death trap she ran directly into. Fox was trying to sort out her feelings. She liked Trevor a great deal and now Shaun made her heart skip at the thought of his touch. Foes she got, feelings were alien to her. Suddenly she was hit with amazing force from the side. She wheeled in mid air to strike but realized much too late that it was because she was in the middle of a life altering trap.

The bleeding man at her feet with fifty or more poison darts stuck in him blinked up at her twice then died with her name in his mouth. There lay Trevor dead in her place. He had saved her from her own stupid mistake. She would not have died of the poison being an eternal and the guardian of the wild, but she would have paid a dear price in pain and misery. A price paid not by her but by dear brave, hansom, loyal Trevor. That was it she knew she loved him suddenly and now he was gone. "SNARL"!

The Red and Micky saw Fox change, and it was not a half change this time but all the way. She had become unhinged at Trevor's loss. There was no saving the guilty, she was judge, jury and the hangman, and they were totally hosed. Fox ripped through the forest not around it. Trees flew to splinters under her wrath.

"Come out and play little goblins" She snarled through clenched teeth, "Fox wants to hugs your throats".

The goblin got the hell out of there of-course they knew death when they seen it. Only one of them thought he could still do some damage so he stayed and put a poison dart in Fox neck, she went to one knee and he rushed out of hiding to plunge his short sword into her hairy back, since she was injured.

To his horror, she turned her head and her yellow-orange eyes danced with death, only not hers. The poison dart was between her sharp teeth. He had a sliver of time before she plunged the dart into his left eye, but not to kill him. No, he was to feel a great deal of pain prior to a bad death was granted.

It would be suicide to interfere with Fox right now and that bastard had it coming so the Red left him to his punishment. It was then that he realized Micky was not next to him or even near by, so The Red tried sensed him out.

At the prone still figure of Trevor, Micky knelt and examined his friend. "Damn, my lad you're in a terrible way". Micky reached into the out and yanked Shaun out. He was beyond angry. Micky acted as if he did not see it.

"I need you to ask yer wee burdy to cry a tear on Trevor there, it could save his life".

"He looks dead to me" Shaun said plainly. He held up a quick hand before Micky could protest. "I don't need to ask the bird to help, if Trevor lives I can intensify his spark and rekindle his light". He raised his hand and tiny flames of a sort that Micky had never seen the like of before danced in Shaun's fingers, then seemed to escape into Trevor's mouth ears, eyes. It was a strange sight to behold indeed. Shaun put his hand on Trevor and said good journey my friend. He turned to Micky, touched his shoulder, turned in a snap movement and was gone.

The Leprechaun was about to reach into the out and get Shaun to ask the Phoenix to help Trevor, because obviously Shaun did not help as much as he believed. He stopped because Trevor took a painful breath and croaked out "FOX" then started coughing and convulsing. Micky was not sure if he should touch Trevor, or to leave him be. Trevor decided for him.

"Get me off the bloody ground and give me ma rifle Mick" Trevor growled in a hoarse tone, grabbing Micky's coat.

"Very well lad" said Micky. He grabbed Trevor by the arms and picked him up with a strength that belied his size.

Trevor could not stand on his own; but he was trying anyway. Micky snatched up the rifle and gave it to Trevor. They walked slowly in the direction that Shaun and Fox had gone. There was a sudden burst of wind and the Red had them both airborne hurdling east in pursuit. Trevor seemed hot in the Red's claw, and being a dragon, he did not usually notice heat. Trevor was noticeably hot, too hot for any human to live.

"He were dead Red, and that fire playing Shaun put fire into Trevor, now he is barning" Micky told the Dragon.

"I am not deaf you arse, you know I kin hear ya. I am not dead only ill lads. Find Fox if you can my giant flying friend" Trevor graveled out.

The chase through the county side and the woods was going at a break neck pace. The goblins were trying to jump into the out but for some reason all the exits and inlets were blocked or closed to them. They were as baffled as they were terrified. The man-ling was after them and they were loosing ground to him with every step. Goblins were not used to being afraid, as a race they were pretty fierce and fearless. However, this was insane, this human was more powerful than Malfeezanz and twice as mad.

The woodlands were full of malice, none of it was from the goblins, if the human was bad, the witch girl was worse and she was pissed beyond all reason and out for blood...theirs.

Shaun was beyond angry; he was once again completely insane and burning. If were not for the Phoenix the atmosphere would be burning. The flamed creature was absorbing the reign of fire coming off the irate man. He was following the goblins not to protect them; he frankly could give a shit about them. However, the man was his friend and mental equal. Yes, Phoenix are a really intelligent old race, there is very little known about them because they shun attention. Only a precious few have ever heard the voice of the Phoenix; and of them only one has ever lived to enjoy the privilege. You see it is usually at the point of your death that you hear the voice, and it is as beautiful as it is deadly. Shaun hears the voice of the Phoenix plain as day; it may be the only thing keeping his soul from tipping into the abyss.

The forest looked like a pile of toothpicks behind Fox. She was a bulldozer, ripping the forest a new one, if you know what I mean. She was rivaling Shaun's fury in sheer raw Aggression. The prey were beating feet and to their credit she had not caught them. They had never been pursued by this hunter killer before, escape was impossible! She meant to kill all these bastards for Trevor. In addition, not just the ones here but all of them everywhere. She had become unhinged at the loss of Trevor. The depth of her despair would be shared she vowed to all who put the stamp of death on him.

"If we don't find a portal to the out we are dead. I cannot go on much longer and the Man and the monster that follows him are gaining on us. We could evade them, but that damn witch woman is dogging us every step. If we turn to evade one the other will catch and kill us" said the goblin leader.

It was too late when they realized what happened. The goblins were hemmed in. They were caught between Shaun and Fox with nowhere to escape.

"ROAR"!

The sound was the last a fringe goblin heard as Fox decapitated him, and tossed his body like a frisbee at the rest of the goblins. They pulled their weapons just as she attacked them. She did not come at them like a hunter, but as a monster, straight on without any caution or care for her person or soul.

The carnage in the clearing in front of Shaun made him step up his pace. Fox was covered in blood. Shaun could not tell if it was hers or theirs but the ground was dyed red with blood from the onslaught. The Goblins were over matched, but they were not going into that good night peacefully. They were fighting as if their lives depended on it...because it did. Goblins dip their blades in poison to assure a kill when they fight a foe. So, even if they loose and die; the enemy will not live to enjoy their defeat. It is brilliant and cowardly at the same time.

"ENOUGH" growled the Dragon. The ground shook as Red Storm slammed into the ground.

The shockwave knocked everyone flat on their ass. Fox was on her feet in an instant and blind with fury at being stopped in the middle of the murders. Nonetheless, Red stopped her. She drove her already healing body back into the mix of injured goblins. Some of them were trying to get away but Shaun burst instantly into flames and began to shout.

"Oh no you don't scum!" Shaun screamed as white hot flames leapt from his left hand and engulfed the area that the goblins were trying to escape through.

One lone goblin was sneaking up behind Fox who was grappling with three goblins. The idiot should have been making a better attempt at stealth. Fox sent him to his maker with a flashed elbow to the skull. A loud report was heard over the den.

"Hey love (cough) save at-least one who can still speak, for the love of Saint Nick" Trevor spat.

"TREVOR" growl Fox!

CHAPTER 19: TROUBLES AT HOME.

In the office of the Irish Prime minister, all chaos had broken out. The latest sightings of monsters, elves or sprites were taking their toll on the population. Panic was rampant in the street of Dublin. Petty differences were forgotten and the Humans began to form bonds and militia to fight off the vicious monsters and capture the timid ones.

Dan Lowe was in the midst of trying to explain that non dangerous creatures should be left in peace or all the magical beings may turn on humanity. Elves were already helping fight the trolls and ghouls side by side with men. Fairies and sprites were attempting to keep the brownies and wraiths away from children and old folks, who might get attacked.

"What if a dragon comes to town eh, what then Mr. Lowe" asked an angry man? "What the bloody hell will you do then; make more speeches while we die in the glens"!

"I hope to GOD almighty that does not happen folks, but we have to deal with what we can, and a dragon is out of our hands" Dan said calmly.

"Maybe not but that is not a major issues gentlemen" said a tiny silk voice. "Dragons will not attack man, or any lesser creatures. They are the oldest of all the magical kingdoms citizens. They are power, magic and fire all bound together. They are our royalty, and all kneel to their wisdom and grace. Only, T'relth is to despise, should you see the great black nightmare and his minions on the move should you flee with all haste".

"Who might you be teeny tiny friend" Dan asked.

A rustle on the desk caught all of their eyes at the same time as a red and gold fairy fluttered forth. A few hands reached out but Dan stopped them with a hard look. A gesture the tiny one did not miss.

Smiling. "I am Arkai of the Golden burst family. We are at your service. My counsel is freely given, yet I would think carefully before you do not heed it, for doom will surely follow" She said sweetly.

"Do you know Mickalean, tiny friend" Dan asked her.

"Yes"

"Well, can you help us find him? He is with Trevor and they seek out the Yank that knows how to stop all of this" Dan said in earnest.

(Giggling)

"Silly man, you ask the impossible, from the impossible, about the impossible" Arkai said ever so sweetly as not to offend.

"I donna understand ya, Arkai, please explain what all of that meant" Dan said while silencing the small crowd with an index finger pointing at his eyes, then his ears.

There was no sound but the traffic squall and children playing across the street on the well-groomed lawns. The people wanted to ask a thousand questions to the tiny speaker. Dan, however was not about to loose the train and line of his thought by some stupid ass query. Rather, he wanted his questions answered in a certain order to help strengthen his position at present. Never let it be said that Dan Lowe was a fool.

"Gladly Dan; First, you seek the ONE or yank as you say. He is the reason we are all awake now" Arkai said.

"Wait, Awake"?

"Yes (giggles), we have always been here, we simply were hidden from your eyes while we rested the centuries away. When the One called out to the Magik and it came, we awoke. All of us, good or bad, small or huge. We came forth and you have seen us. That very fact means we are in your minds and hearts, so we are strong in this world again and will not sleep the great rest again in your great grand kid's life times. You must understand your acceptance of our being here and now makes it impossible to undo what has been done. More, the One who called out to the power is intermeshed with The Pure Flame of the Inferno. He is mad with grief, and that has made him the destroyer. Micky, is old and wise even by a dragons standard. He knows as well as I that this cannot be stopped, only controlled Dan. ONLY CONTROLLED" Arkai laughed "So you see impossible all around and complete".

"Shit" Dan grumbled as he sat heavily in his high backed chair behind his desk. Silent whispers went around his huge lonely office and hard desperate looks as well.

"Is there no hope" an older woman asked in soft corn silk way?

"There is always hope. The Phoenix rides the shoulder and the soul of the One. Among the realms and kingdoms, a Phoenix is sacred; they are the only creature other than the dragons that GOD gave the gift of fire. Not regular fire, the fire of creation or damnation. Only the LORD our GOD has control over them. There is nothing we know of that can stand against them, and their judge of you is final" Arkai said.

"What hope is that" Dan asked confused.

"Come Humans to the window and I will show you" Arkai said with a finality.

The sun was setting and the star began to dust the heavens.

The sunburst in the East was breath taking. Odd though is seemed to shimmer ever so slightly at times, like heat waves over a hot highway.

"Do you not see it humans" Arkai asked?

"Please tell me what I am looking for" Dan said a bit sharp, not looking away from the sunset?

"You will know soon enough" Arkai explain.

A shiver shook her tiny body for an instant.
Dan noticed it and wondered what made his brave new ally so nervous and tight? She was old he thought. Not that she looked old, quite the opposite she was a mini goddess. Her golden edged wings and red hue hair and white skin made her likely the most beautiful female Dan had ever seen. It was supernatural how lovely she was. Sadly, she was really, really tiny.

"There, watch the horizon "Arkai said

Dan and all of the people did just that, they watched where their guide told them. A moment later, they did not need to ask what made Arkai shiver. A blast of the richest red-orange flame danced across the entire sky right past the horizon toward them. Then a visual tap came the flame were simply gone.

"That is the hope, the future out there. It is the Phoenix absorbing the One's flame before it burns the world. The amazing flame is the man you seek, the one you think has some answers for your issues, and the second is the guardian who watches over him. He is then twice as impossible to stop or reason with or yes Dan, kill" Arkai said with a dirty look.

The prime Minister sat down again hard. He brought his eyes up to look into Arkai's, in that instant he knew she could read his mind. A more important revelation came unexpectedly to him.

136

"You must never tell another living soul that your mind is open to me Dan, and I can speak directly into it. I am unique among my people in this ability; it is very rare and dangerous for me. If it were known, I would be killed by even the goodly creatures. They would fear me and my ability to break into their minds. It is a great crime to listen to another's thoughts; it is death to interject your own into their mind. One word of caution Dan, I can kill you with a thought. That is my power. Fear no enemy when I am with you, for I can know and stop any assault on you before it can come to fruition" Arkai whispered softly in Dan's mind.

Dan sat there just looking at Arkai. He could feel the truth of her words and the power, so immense behind them. He was positively drunk from the minor touch of the ocean this tiny woman had. He was not sure if fear or elation was the correct emotion. He decided caution and admiration were correct. Arkai felt this and was satisfied they were partners and friends from here on out.

The crowd in Dan's office was asked to leave. They had silently witnessed the exchange but did not understand it at all. They did know, however that something was exchanged and it was likely important to the world and not just their corner of it.

DRAGON & FIRE TALE

CHAPTER 20: THE KEEP

In the Out, regular rules of reality do not apply. Gravity, weights, measures were just words with no more importance than that. Usually a trip through the Out was an instant travel movement. Ayla noticed at once there was something vague and wholly wrong here and she said this softly to Kala. Kamy was being carried by Rolf, who became fully human prior to setting foot into the out. T'relth actually waited for him to change before departing. Kamy was both terrified into immobility and fascinated by Rolf, She was a prize as human women went, beautiful and witty, though small; she was capable of amazing physical endurance. Rolf chatted her up the whole time as if this was a trip with friends to the park and he was her buddy.

"Why have we been in the Out so long Dragon" Ayla asked none too politely?

"I since in you strength and courage little one, so I am not offend by your rash actions. We are going to my hold or home if you like. None may come here unless I allow it and I do not allow it. We have made a series of jumps my dear, not one as you believe currently" T'relth said to Ayla gently.

"So, Your hiding from him" Kala said Suddenly.

"Who would that be" T'relth asked with a sincere smile?

"My guess is whoever tamed the Phoenix" Kala said flatly and was rewarded with a shocked look from Rolf and the man-dragon.

"How could you know that wretch" Rolf asked in a near snarl.

"Oh, Shut up Rolf. Therefore, you are also not without worth I see girl. You are larger and stronger than your companions are. Yes, exceptionally beautiful as well I should think. I will have to think on you for a time, you may be strong enough and able to carry my child human. Your genes would not spoil the mix either, yes a good woman for my needs" T'relth said smoothly.

Kala was not happy about drawing the dragon's attention to her, quite the opposite actually. Yet, if he continued to think on her and Ayla then the wolf could not kill them. Therefore, her feelings were mixed.

Another serious consideration was Rolf's unhealthy affections toward little Kamy, who was somewhat smitten it would seem with the wolf-man. Ayla was another problem; she was to strong for her own good. These monsters were likely to play hard with her then toss her broken husk aside with no second thought. It is then going to fall on me she thought to see that does not happen.

"What are you on about girl, pay attention or you might hurt yourself" Thurv said suddenly?

They stepped out finally into the sun of an unfamiliar land. There were miles of green and red swaying fields as the gentle wind nudged them into an eternal dance. The Sky was a rich blue with a smattering of cotton candy clouds begging for a nibble. The air was sweet and clean, carrying with is the smell of wild flowers and life. It was much too nice for the killers who just came to this place.

"Oh how beautiful it is here." Kamy said happily.

"Yes, it is" Rolf answered her as he placed a hand on her bare shoulder.

"Come ladies and gentlemen, this way if you please" T'relth said calmly.

"Or if you don't please either" Kala said in a huff.

Thurv snickered and walked by looking at Kala with what she took to be mirthful acceptance of her comments, perhaps even approval. It did not go unnoticed by Rolf or Mal. It would seem that there was no love among the monster.

"Where is this great Keep you have told us about, that even the RED can't find" Mal asked softly with some concern?

"BEHOLD" T'relth shouted as he raised his hands above his head!

The ground shook and the Earth split open and the air became so hot the girls were having troubles breathing. The man who was really a dragon opened his human mouth and red and black flames burst forth and scorched the ground as it opened up. Some sort of mix of magic and nature cause a fortress to suddenly appear where the burnt area was. It was nearly invisible except for the flames that tickled the sides of it.

(Cough).

"I have not had to do that in a long time, I had forgotten drain on my human form to bring my Keep out. I should like to don my true dragon mantle next time to save time and strength" T'relth said, amused by his coughing fit.

"That is it, the famed Keep of the great Black dragon. We have been comrades for years and I never knew how overblown your idea of this place was until now. I am not impressed" Thurv said plainly. He turned to Rolf to see his impression and could tell he felt the same.

"Looks can be deceiving troll king, come inside my friend" T'relth said, in a silk voice.

The massive troll moved to the Keeps main door, which was huge and made of a strange color shifting metal. He reached out and made an attempt to open the door and enter. He was

141

forceful repelled away the entrance as if shot from a canon.

"Fascinating, may I try the door" Ayla asked suddenly.

Thurv was still smoking as he picked himself up out of the field he was firmly tossed into. T'relth studied the small woman for a moment, as if wondering if she was suicidal. He was caught between wanting to see the results and using her to draw the hated RED into a death trap since his nemesis was following the flaming one who was after Malfeezanz. The goblin that killed his mate.

"No, master. Do not allow her the chance. She is charmed in a way that make the improbable into possible and the crazy...sanity" Mal pleaded.

"It is settle girl, try the door if you but dare to" The dragon said, with a look of wonder.

The tiny human woman walked up to the door fully intending to kill herself. In the way Shaun would go home and not fall into the trap being set for him. Her life was nothing if it cost him his. Ayla reach out without a moment's hesitation and opened the portal. There was not explosion, or magical repulsion that the troll faced. There was only an open portal into the Black's Keep.

"I must watch this one, she is indeed charmed" T'relth whispered to himself.

CHAPTER 21: OF EARTH AND FIRE

The thunder in the distance made the ground shake. There was actually a pleasant sensation for the once lonely being walking across the wilderness toward the thunder. The land called out for him to stop the pain and set right the damage done.

A happy song could be heard across the plains and the animal life joined into the eerie tune without fear. Predators sat beside prey and watched the person walk by as if the world had called a truce and the one person was spreading the good tidings. It must have been much like when Jesus walked the world, where hate was not a thought in the minds of the onlookers. Oh no, heck no, Brick is no God or even the son of the maker. No, he is just blessed as he would say, with Maker give gifts.

"To where do you go Brick" Liri asked from his right shoulder where she sat most of the time caressing his ear?

"We go to heal the world love" Brick said softly so as not to hurt her ears.

There were two goddesses sitting on the shoulders of the biggest man anyone had ever seen. They were a Black hair, blue-eyed angel and her brown haired twin. So gorgeous were the women, they were beyond the words of a poet to describe. The giant was as handsome as he was big. His kindly eyes twinkled as he looked at his tiny passengers. They had an obvious affection growing between them. How impossible that love seemed, and yet, so beautiful to behold despite it.

"There will come a time when you may need to return to Mara and Sayu for safety ladies. I cannot be harmed easily or be injured. I cannot say the same for you two. When I say go you will go" Brick said in his kindly tone.

"We have been harpies Brick for centuries, we are much tougher than you know, and I will not flee your side unless Liri's life is in jeopardy" Sera said "and that my big friend is final"!

(Laughter and giggles)

"Ok, I know when to yield ladies, but seriously there are trash walking the land with their unclean footprints, and the land cries for renewal and protection. Some of these are too powerful to play child's games with. So, you will leave if I say or we go no further together" Brick told them.

   The Giant stone grey, blue eyes, blond man stopped and looked at Liri with so much feeling that her skin prickled. She loved him already, silly as that was. Brick looked at Sera more sternly.

"Obey me in this or take your sister and leave me Sera, I will not see you dead. Either, of you" Brick said sounding like a stone mill in the deep ocean. He was as deep as a whale and twice as powerful.

"I give my word gentle Brick, I will obey your order to flee with Liri when you say" Sera promised.

"I do not" Liri said boldly "promise to flee your side if trouble comes. It would surely tear the very heart from my tiny breasts to see you stand alone".

 Hot tears ran from her perfect slightly almond shaped eyes and down onto Brick's neck. He was indestructible and his skin mighty. He however would swear he felt the rain of her tears on his neck and it crushed his mighty heart on his massive chest. Sera and Liri were not blood sisters at birth, but when Sayu
   enslaved them that all changed. It was at the moment that
144

Mara brought back their humanity that they became twins. They were not real angels. Mara; however shaped them in the image of angels, complete with working wings and special gifts. Those gifts seemed to be stronger when they were together, so they were twins. When Liri the softhearted fell in love with the gentleman giant Brick, so did Sera. This was a secret not even Brick knew. So Sera cried when Liri cried, every single time.

"Don't cried angels, please don't" Brick whispered to the tiny objects of his heart.

How lonely had he been, how solitary, always telling himself, that is how he wanted it? He knew that was a lie to mask his longing for a companion or mate. Now, the big moose had two angels and knew happiness that was previously denied to him. He thought himself extremely lucky at this moment. Still, the thought of anyone or thing harming them made his diamond hard skin crawl and his pulse quicken. He took a vow right then, no matter what may come; no harm, on his life would be visited on them...ever!

The land was growing dark and the sky was in a burst of angry reds and oranges. Brick could hear the trees dying and the animals crying for their lost families. He needed to hurry, things were out of control. He had to fix the damage that was his life, his purpose. Brick began to run. The Angels took to the air, because they could tell that Brick was running careful because of them. Once they left his shoulders, Brick really began to run. He tripled his speed inside of 200 yards and was still pulling hard for more top end momentum.

"My; what a powerful runner our boy is" Sera teased Liri.

"Yes, a graceful body, filled with enough strength to do anything" Liri reflected aloud, as much to herself as Sera. Liri knew Sera felt the same love she did for Brick and that brought her comfort in her painful shyness.

The graceful juggernaut ran day and night with two lovely

angels fluttering around his head keeping up easily. Brick
reflected to himself, that the girls were not affected by the pace
so far and seemed not to tire at all, or become hungry, which he
was at the moment. Therefore, at the realization he was hungry
Brick tossed the breaks on and stopped.

The girls banked hard, flew right up to his face, and looked at
him in a quizzical way.

"Maker, you two are so lovely" Brick said, surprising him and
them both, since he did not share his feeling easily. He blushed.
"I am hungry girls and I need food, so I stopped".

   The three travelers looked around and they saw a nearby
orchard with a tiny human man of extremely advanced age
working at the edge of it. Brick smiled and walk toward the
fellow.

The old man saw Brick but must have thought his eyes were tired
so he did not react much. Well, until Brick got down low and
spoke to him softly.

"Excuse me sir, may I have the use of your orchards to feel
myself and my friends" Brick said as sweetly as he could.

"Hell NO" the man shouted. He was somewhat deaf the girls
thought.

   The angels landed by the old man and he was nearly blind as
well by their guess. Liri placed her soft silky hands over the
man's eyes and Sera put her hands over his ears and they
hummed in harmony. The lil man tried to resist at first, but then
he became aware that his back pain, leg, arm and stomach pains
were all gone. The angels stepped back and removed their soft
hands.

   The man stood as still as a marble statue in an art collection
   for a few long minutes. He opened his eyes and looked at
146

Brick; he started for a tick, and then recovered. He turned his gaze to the girls for the first time and he lost his breath. He fell to his knees and cried.

"OH dear GOD, what did we do wrong Sera" Liri asked in horror! She was on the verge of a serious cry.

"NO, NO (sob, cough) you did everything so, so right" The farmer cried with so much emotion as his voice cracked.

"Come on now farmer, your body should be young and strong again, I saw to the return of your vitality myself" Sera said as she sat down by the man. She reached out and took his hand.

"Real, you're real. I can feel your hands on mine. Am I dead? Is that why you angels have come, and is he the devil here to fight for my soul" The farmer asked?

"No, he is a giant. We are not God's Angels farmer, we only have some of the gifts they might have, we can heal injuries or in your case degeneration. We fixed your sight, hearing and health in return for helping our giant" Liri said sweetly.

"I can't', you see. I make my living off the fruit and if he eats all of it I will not be able to pay my bills and live" the farmer said apologetically.

"Oh, that is no problem sir. I am a guardian of the wild places, keeper of the lands. I can grow anything. Let me show you" Brick said.

The giant looked to where the farmer had been toiling hard to plant some tiny fruit tree saplings in the rocky earth. Brick touched the ground with his left index figure and began to sing a happy song. The ground opened, water filled the holed from below, the saplings roots popped out of the sacks they were in, and into the holes they went. Brick sang a slightly different melody and the trees, began to grow and fruit buds began to show at once. Inside of a few short minutes, the farmer had five more mid-sized trees laden fruit. Brick only smiled down at the man. Then he climbed back onto his huge feet and went to main orchard where the trees were in bad need of water. Brick just smiled

The farmer watched Brick dig twelve-foot deep channels from the river to the orchard by hand. The giant sang or hummed the entire time and where he went plants began to grow. When the irrigation work was done, Brick sat down by the farmer and sang the most beautiful song anyone had ever heard. The trees had a sudden life that the farmer in his ninety-three years had never witnessed before. Fruit fell off the trees into neat piles for one hour only. Brick stopped singing at that point.

"What was that song son" the little farmer asked?

"It was the song of making my friend. I asked the trees to make fruit for me in return for the water and life I have traded them. They said yes" Bricks smiled as he explained.

"Why did you stop at one hour" the farmer wanted to know?

"I can't ask for more than a short burst of making without hurting them" Brick said softly in a reverent voice.

"It will not be enough for you Brick" The farmer said. "Do you want a cow to eat or a pig"?

"No thanks, I do not eat animals sir" Brick said.

"Well me either but I owe you" the farmer said.

"Non-sense, we helped each other, we are square" Brick chuckled.

The road was more enjoyable for the angels who got to see yet another incredible thing about the Brick they loved. How many life times of secrets, must he have all balled up wanting to be shared. They intended in finding out. It would be fun to tease it out of him.

The sky was getting hotter the farther inland Brick went. He could feel the land screaming with insanity for respite. Once again, the pressure built inside of the giant until he had to run to make it go away.

DRAGON & FIRE TALE

CHAPTER 22: LESSONS.

The fate of the world was being decided by warriors willing to risk it all for what they believed in. Whether good or evil they were all giving it their all to prove dominion over their foe. There was a problem with that; the sides were evenly matched at present, causing an everlasting stalemate.

Sayu watched the sleeping form of her new companion and not for the first time wondered if she had chosen correctly by releasing her from her life as a harpy. Mara was so beautiful and kind. She made Sayu feel ashamed of her actions in the past. Why, Sayu kept asking that question herself. Why, had she given power and Beauty back to Mara? The power was new, but the beauty was not. It was only what Sayu had, in jealousy stolen from the girl. Therefore, once again why had she, the greatest sorcerer in the world let her go and enchanted her to boot. Baffled and weary Sayu lay on the bed by Mara. The sleepy youth rolled over, put her arm around the sorcerer, and pulled her near. Sayu just gave a wry smile and drifted into a content rest.

Flames flashed thru the sky in the distance, yelling that power and evil had drawn out a champion. That champion was drunk with passion; that much Mara could feel in her bones. Mara unfolded her snow-white wings and leaned out the window to let the wind catch her. She was frightened, but the call of the sky whispered in her mind to come and play with us. The sensation of the wind in your hair and the tickle of air currents teasing the feathers on her back was a simple paradise to Mara. She reveled in her new body, in addition, her ability to soar into the heavens. Mara knew she would have to leave soon and help her little sisters in the trials to come. She did not want to leave Sayu, but knew not how to ask the powerful woman to join her.

Mara was not sure if she loved Sayu, or just admired her.

"Mara where are you darling" Sayu called.

"I am out here Mistress" Mara called into the window.

The lithe girl, who was over a thousand years old, ran to the window to find her creation floating just out of reach in front of the big gold framed side bedroom window. Mara had torn her outer gown off and only retained her sheer slip, so she was free to flex her wing muscles uninhibited.

I wonder if I could kill her, just shoot her out of the sky with a lightning bolt. Alternatively, maybe just freeze her in place and let the ground impact finish my work for me? Sayu startled herself by digging her nails into her arm until blood flowed freely down her bare legs. Mara pinned her wings to her back like a cape and dropped into the room. She grabbed Sayu's arm away from the attacking nails of her other hand, and kissed the bleeding arm.

"Now that is better. All the damage is repaired and you will have no scar" Mara said with a sad look on her face.

"I don't know what came over me, I am sorry Mara for bothering you with my petty troubles" Sayu said, once again surprising herself with the depth of her feeling for the girl. Sayu had injured herself for thinking of harming her companion unjustly. Mara came to Sayu; tenderly fix the damage with love and caring. Sayu saw all too clearly, what the problem was where Mara was concerned. She cared for the child and wanted to be cared for in return. This was not normal for Sayu, who was selfish and cruel.

"Sayu my dear one, I have to ask you to listen and forgive me. I will need to leave soon to add my sisters. They will have great need and face great peril that they cannot handle on their own. I can't let them die for my lack of action," Mara said sadly.

The witch said nothing for a long awhile she just held Mara's hand, while looking out the window at the breath taking view she had enjoyed for more than a thousand years.

(Giggle)

"Then my precious one, I shall go with you, for if you would face danger for your two sisters; I will not let you face such a peril alone. I am loathed to admit it but you have changed me for the better. I doubt if I could make the total sweet transition to be you Mara, however I find I want to make you love me for the efforts I undertake on your behalf" Sayu admitted.

"You need do nothing more for me than be with me, although Sayu I would be glad of your mighty powers to help me protect my sisters" Mara said sweetly.

Sayu did not say it aloud but she cared nothing for the other angels, and she would only use her magic to preserve Mara's life. If the others died so be it, she would spend no tears.

"Come child let us bath you, you are still covered in perspiration and you clothing is soiled with my foolish blood" Sayu said gently to her companion.

The girls walked into the bathhouse inside of the castle, which Sayu had built. Sayu usually used it to entertain men, which later she killed by sucking out their vitality, thus she stayed young without having to use magic. Mara prepared the bath mixing cold water with the water heated by a hot spring that ran deep under the structure until it felt perfect. She beckoned to Sayu to come to her so that she may undress her. Sayu returned the favor. They slipped into the hot scented water together and rubbed each other's back with rose bud soap. It was then that Sayu noticed that Mara's wings were gone, her back was flawlessly bare.

"Where are your wings Mara" Sayu asked?

(Innocent giggle)

"I put them away Sayu, when I don't need them I can simple fold them and they return to my inner self until I have need of them again" Mara explained. "Did you not make me that way"?

Sayu was genuinely surprised; she had no idea at all how this could be. The magic spell or spells to accomplish such a feat would be very powerful and hard to constantly maintain.

"Actually no darling, I didn't. I am not at all sure how you are able to do it. It seems to just be so, as if it were your destiny or divine right from the Maker," Sayu said.

"Are you not the Maker" Mara asked confused.

"Heaven no child, I am a sorceress; I can use and play with magic, but the one who rules us all created me. GOD" Sayu explained. "I have been alive a great span of years and the only absolute in this world is that the maker is with us, watching and weighing the good and bad in us all. We shall all be judge when our time comes".

"Why do you look suddenly so sad Sayu" Mara asked?

"Oh sweet child, I have done great evil, I have taken that which was not mine to take. I have shown the maker no reason to judge me worthy. One day I will hear the Phoenix sing...and be no more" Sayu said with tears in her almond eyes.

"Don't cry, I will help you find your way". We will face the Phoenix together and you will be judge fairly by our maker, and go to your reward with joy in your heart" Mara said with so much love it made Sayu's heart swell with joy.

The next morning the women packed all the items they would need for a long and possible fatal journey to the place where the Earth was scorched.

Thus, they went forward into a new life for Sayu and a first real adventure for Mara. Sayu could see her salvation in Mara's goodness. Mara saw in Sayu a heart wanting desperately to be saved. They quietly decided they would each save the other no matter what the cost to themselves. Therefore, the journey began.

DRAGON & FIRE TALE

CHAPTER 23: PERSONAL GAIN

The afternoon was going slowly and Orrin was not able to concentrate on the subject that he had chosen to master this period. Orrin had long ago mastered the fine art of absorbing knowledge. However, not this day, his thoughts were troubled and he could feel the mega powered fight in the distance. The very air danced with magical energies on the high level of dragon combat. Surely, no other creatures could muster up this kind of raw magical might. Orrin could not shake the thought that this was the power of the mortal that he faced in the human village a month ago.

A bird landed on the window of his study and cheeped at him. Orrin was verse in the voices of nature. For as an Elf mage it was second nature to him.

The bird said (I bring you greetings mighty Elf and I am to inform you that T'relth requests your presence for a meeting for mutual gratification. You must send a reply, and the answer will be yes).

Orrin was no child or lackey to be ordered about by anyone. He was more than a tad put off by the tiny bird's relayed message. Yet, he had to admit his own intrigue at the summons. Therefore, he decided his course and took it.

Reverting to the birds tongue he said (I except, where am I to meet this master of yours, and when)?

The bird chirped once, then once more. He was not speaking; Orrin realized a moment too late to stop the events as they played out. The wizard found himself transported across a great vast space in a millisecond. The elf found himself out in the open plains of what he believed was Russia.

"Who dares...?" Orrin began, but he gargled the rest in shock away into the vault of better judgment.

"Hello little elf mage" Said a booming voice.

"Oh Shit" Orrin proclaimed with a sour look on his face.

"Thank you for accepting my invitation".

"Invitation, how generous you are with meaningless terms. Why not just send word that you wished to see me, instead of paltry trickery," Orrin said rather dryly.

"Oh very well Orrin" T'relth said

"So what does the great Black dragon of evil need that I could provide that he could not" Orrin asked in honest inquiry?

"A fair question, yes I should think. Once you faced a human who could manipulate fire and tame a Phoenix. I wish you to kill him," T'relth said flatly in answer.

"No".

"No, you refuse me" T'relth asked?

"No, he could not tame a Phoenix, they, as you well know, mind, and heel toe for the maker and only the maker. So, I say no, it is not so" Orrin said.

"Would you stake your life on it," T'relth asked?

The elf mage walked over to the edge of the step he was standing on and gazed out over the plains. This was a problem for him. He had been plagued with the feeling that the damnable human was gaining more power all the time and he was somehow responsible for the rumbling of old magic in the world. Orrin had to figure this out. What he needed no time; was the Black, this one he knew and understood. Why then would one as omnipotent as the Black need him to snuff a human? Orrin feared only the RED; he was not to be trifled with in anyway. The Black as long as you kept a tab on him, was manageable.

"What does my old friend need of me? Wait, what will you do for me if I should decide to accept the task" Orrin asked slyly?

"I offer you your life, don't think you can pressure me elf," The dragon snarled.

"Oh do piss off, as if you could take me so easily" Orrin said as he slipped into a mid-phase, which would keep him from any harm.

The Black did not notice this and blew a spout of fire down on the elf, which just stood there looking bored. T'relth saw this was not the way to deal with the knowledge hungry elf. Therefore, he tried another approach.

"Fine, I will share a black dragon magic scroll, when you kill the human" T'relth said.

"Nay, you will give it to me now, if it is authentic, then the human is forfeit, agreed" Orrin said?

"Done" T'relth exclaimed in amusement!

The Black produced an actual ancient scroll from the black dragon horde. Orrin was quite pleased. What the Black did not know was Orrin had the greatest joy in the fact that he had a photographic memory and total recall reproduction. Therefore, once he looked at the scroll, he had the knowledge for life. The dragon thought to offer, and then withdraw the offer of the scroll after Orrin had completed his task. Orrin knew this and played the dragon for a fool. Orrin was very old, despite his outward appearance and the dragon had forgotten this fact to his utter stupidity.

"A fine trade, I find that it is as you said it would be. I am engaged, the human will fall" Orrin said blithely.

"Then it is done mage, you will kill the human and bring his remains to me" T'relth said.

"You may have whatever is left, if there is anything left to have" Orrin answered.

The answer actually pissed off the dragon that was used to getting his way in everything. The elf was not his servant he reminded himself. No serious threat to him but still very dangerous to deal with. T'relth had other plans to attend to so he bid the mage ado and stepped into the out vanishing.

The mage stood for a while and considered the task ahead of him and why a dragon, this dragon that was next in line as far as power went within the dragon clans. Yet, he turned to him to put the human down. Orrin decide to go observe this human and see what the big production was about.

CHAPTER 24: BIG HELL NO

What was left of the goblins was not much and nasty to boot. The prevailing smell was burnt flesh and other various smells related to burning items. Therefore, there was no stench of dead goblin reek, because of a literal baptism by fire.

"TREVOR" Fox roared.

The adventurer was still pretty messed up from the goblin poison and perhaps the enchanted fire that kept the poison from killing Trevor did more than it's fair share of the damage Trevor now sported. Trevor was so overjoyed at being able to still breathe, he thought his chips were cashed. However, Shaun made the impossible happened, he had intervened and saved Trevor's life. The adventurer had thought that Shaun had no regard for him at all, perhaps he was wrong about Shaun, but he did not think so.

"Hey there Love, not dead yet I spose" Trevor said to Fox as she jumped next to him. He smiled and looked her over. "Oiy, I like the fur baby, it suits ya".

"Cheeky fool, you could have been killed, your only human, be more careful" Fox growled at Trevor.

Fox was shocked when Trevor reached up and pulled her down into his embrace. Her first instinct was to pull away and smite him. Fox let her body shift in tight to his and became her softer nearly human form. She kissed him back and let herself want him as bad as she ever denied it priorly. Fox did not want to hold back anymore. She finally gave in to the desire she felt but could not understand. Trevor had nearly died without her letting him know that she loved him. He was a human as well; life was strangely ironic these days.

"What now lad, ye killed all the Goblin'ers," Micky said in his broke Irish tones.

"I want to lie down and sleep Mick, but I am so deeply angry and frustrated right at this moment I am not sure it would help" Shaun exclaimed.

The juggernaut that was Shaun, a human fire elemental, looked worse than the goblins Fox mutilated. Never had Micky seen a man so badly in need of rest and joy. Maker help anyone who crossed this man. Shaun was so close to a psychotic meltdown, than even the Red was worried about what he could do to prevent the end of days. It was a fine thing that the mighty Phoenix watched over the boy, balancing him out. It seemed at time that the flame bird siphoned off the madness as well as the fire when Shaun was about to go supernova.

"WHERE IS SHE" Screamed a suddenly flame covered Shaun?!

Fire jumped onto everything in the area. Micky tossed up a null barrier around Trevor, Fox and himself so they would not be turned to ash, as the world began to burn.

"STOP THAT," bellowed a huge voice just before a massive fist caught Shaun in the chest, sending him hurdling into a pine tree.

Trevor looked up with a start at the biggest man he had ever seen. He was all over grey with bright blond hair and perfect teeth, which were gritted. The giants blue eyes were riveted to where Shaun laid in a heap, with obviously fractured bones. Fox snarled like an animal and would have lunged to attack but she was wrapped up with Trevor and he would not let go.

"Oh Shoit" Micky said.

The giant made to approach and press the attack he started when...

"ROOOOOOOAR"!!!!

The RED dropped right point blank into the giant's handsome face and made the giant back pedal.

"Coward, you attack without warning against a human who is in my charge" The Red snarled so loud that the sky trembled. Argast snapped his tail around and gave the giant a good cuff in the face.

The impact of the blow would have killed a lesser giant; Brick was hurt and smarting but would live. He was still at a loss why the Red was attacking him. Did the dragon not see the human was killing the world? Brick had come to heal the land, but he must stop the man at all costs. The Red made that impossible.

"Liri are you ok," Sera asked excitedly?

"Yes, sister I am well. Brick are you ok," Liri asked concerned?

"I am ok girls, now hide, we are in trouble" Brick said softly.

"Why don't you just beat up the dragon and then crush the man" Sera asked?

"You cheap shit, back jumping bastard" came a voice behind the Red! "You want to sucker punch me Mother f…"

The Red cut short what was being said with a warning roar at the giant. Brick misunderstood the Red's clear warning of danger to late to stop what happened.

The Phoenix landed on Shaun's shoulder. It placed one talon on each side of Shaun's neck and spread his flaming wings. Shaun put his hands out directly under each wings. Then the most startling thing Micky and Argast had ever seen happened suddenly. The man and Phoenix became one.

"Oh Maker, I am in serious trouble" Brick said. "Get the hell out of here, run" he screamed at the angels.

The living firebird moved at the speed of light and hit the giant with a force that shook the entire county at once. There was not witty banter, and threats, just pain. Lots and lots of serious pain.

"Fox save the girls, love" Trevor said pointing at the angels, "They are not part of this.

Like lightning Fox move in a blur. She grabbed the girls and dove furiously back into the barrier, which Micky was having a hard time hold open under Shaun's assault. Fox started to say your safe when Sera decked her.

(Laughter)

"Sweetie, you gotta be kidding, I have fought dragons, giants and trolls, You don't have shit on that punch baby, now sit" Fox told Sera, the knocked her on her butt. Fox looked at Liri and motioned for her to also sit, though not unkindly.

The old magic in the Red screamed to be let out, and since Argast could think of no way to stop this madness, the dragon did something that even Micky was surprised to see. Ice.

(Hum, rum, secum) The dragon chanted this three times. At the finish of the last syllable, the ground and air became frozen instantly. This would not and could not stop Shaun and the Phoenix on his back. However, it did cause a pause in the action, and most likely save a giant funeral bill.

"Amazing Red, simply amazing" Shaun said with a burning crackling voice. "OK, Release me my friend".

The Phoenix closed it's wings and hopped onto Shaun's right shoulder, which effectively ended the fire storm assault. Brick was trying to get up. Shaun move like Fox's twin and hit the giant on the chin so hard Brick went down dazed.

"Now we're even you prick" Shaun spat in Brick's bruised face.

Micky dropped the shield and looked at Brick up close. He hummed and ha-ed a few times and gave a whistle, then shook his head at Brick, like a father to an idiot child.

"Be thank'n the maker the Red was here to save yer bum lad," Micky told Brick.

"Oh my poor Brick" Liri said as she healed his lacerations.

"You're not a nice person are you," Sera said to Shaun.

Micky grabbed Sera's hand and Liri's and made them both sit by Brick while he told Shaun's story to them. Both angels cried. Brick hung his mighty head in shame for his part in this sad tale.

"A terrible burden, but he must stop killing the world" Brick said extremely loudly.

"What is your dysfunction amigo now" Shaun asked in a huff?

"Your tirades are killing the world, they must stop. The planet needs to be healed" Brick growled unafraid right down in Shaun's angry face.

"Is that what this is all about" Shaun asked, "you attacked me over that, did you ever think to just asked for help, you ignorant jackass"?

"Well...er, no, sorry" Brick said sheepishly.

"Do you know how to fix what you say is broken giganto" Shaun asked?

"Yes; I am a forest giant and the caretaker of the wild places.

If I get the time to heal the world I can, but I have my limited. Once my strength is gone, so is the healing".

The scene that day would never be forgotten by all who stood witness to it. Shaun placed his hand on Bricks forehead and smiled. The Phoenix came to Shaun's summons and landed on his right forearm. All three began to glow like a rainbow.

The land around and under the giants feet began to grow grass, wild flowers and new life. Saplings that were a burnt up mess were now huge and powerful looking redwoods, well just as big. The waterless valleys they had passed now had springs and lakes full of fish and plant life. Shaun's eyes were open the whole time unblinking, as if he were seeing a far off place, which of-course he was. Brick's eyes were closed and he was covered in sweat. The Phoenix sat still and glowed like the sun for Shaun. All of a sudden, Shaun stopped the whole thing. Brick fell on his face sound asleep. The Phoenix took to wing to hunt. Shaun just smiled at the giant and began to walk into the forest to continue his quest.

"What the hell just happened" Sera asked to no certain person?

"Well if I live another thousand years, I don't think I will ever see the like of that again. What just happened lass is Shaun used the giant's knowledge, the Phoenix power and his own will to reshape the damage earth to complete health and vitality," Micky explain with a chuckle.

Elsewhere Sayu shot bolt upright and jerked her head around to look off to the west where the missing angels went with the handsome giant. A blind fear or more likely anxiety came over Sayu. She did not understand why she was so upset; she did not care about those two. Alternatively, perhaps she was wrong and she did care deep down. No matter she decided that she must hurry to their side and defend them for Mara's sake.

CHAPTER 25: EPIPHANY

The elf mage tried to jump from the out into the forest near Shaun so he could whack him from behind and be done with it. Orrin would quietly collect the corpse and drop it off for the Silly lizard to play with or eat as he preferred.

The scene in the clearing just a few yards from where Orrin popped forth from the out, was not what the elf had envisioned. A mixed blood giant of incredible might just tagged a tiny human in the chest. So much for him, Orrin thought. A sudden movement caught the elf's eyes.

"God dammit" Orrin growled between his teeth to himself. "Not the Red, not him. Oh, what were the chances of this? The bastard of a black dragon knew all along that the Red was involved. He thought to set up me for the kill after I snuffed the human. I will pay T'relth back for this honor by bringing the Red to his door step"!

Orrin was not finished with his revelations. For in the next instant Fox the Goddess of the wilds was there and grabbed two girls that looked like a cross between a butterfly and a human. Angels, the word popped into his mind. Now Orrin was bothered. Was the Maker trying to balance something out, if so should Orrin leave well enough alone? Nevertheless, what was this, there was a powerful barrier placed around the girls, Fox, and human male and...

"Mickalean" Orrin shouted aloud in anger.

The elf master mage, the greatest elf sorcerer of all time had never know defeat or a revival in power or magical knowledge until the fated day when the festering wound that is Patrick Savage Mickalean crossed his path. That day Orrin learned the meanings of doubt and self-evaluation, for Mickalean pushed Orrin to new heights of magic use, and new realms of magic. So mighty was their contestation, that in the end Orrin believed Mickalean had perished and Mickalean believed the same of the elf.

"This changes everything, I cannot face the Red and Mickalean," Orrin growled in frustration. "But wait, what is this, the human rises after a direct hit from the giant"?

The view the mage had while Shaun tossed Brick a beaten, afforded him time to analyze the strength of the gathered enemies. Ok, strictly speaking, they were not his enemies, yet, they were much more than mere opponents. Therefore, Orrin being one of the greatest scholars the planet has ever know, reverted to student mode and studied them in every possible way to find a way to break them down. In this way, Orrin had beaten all of his foes, except Mickalean; well and the damned human.

The elf was well hidden from the ensuing battle, which was one sided pretty much from the cradle to the grave. Orrin was shocked to see the Phoenix merge it's essence with the man. Why would a near god demean itself to help a mere human? It was a senseless. Still, Orrin watched in amazement as the giant tried everything from brute strength to earth magic on the man-Phoenix. Nothing worked; nothing at all. He was unstoppable. It was when the Red use old deep magic to bring forth a freeze that the man paused.

He stood there smiling and acknowledged to the dragon that he was finished, the giant had taken enough to learn from his mistake. The Phoenix disengorged the man of the sacred fire, flew up to his shoulder, and watched.

The giant who named himself Brick explained the reason for his assault. All listened as the giant told of the damage the

168

DRAGON & FIRE TALE

human did to the planet and the extreme need to heal the wrong. The human chewed out Brick for not just asking.

Orrin was about to take his shot at ending the human, when the final major surprise of the day and possibly Orrin's life came. The man placed a hand on the giant's head and held up his arm and commanded the Phoenix to him, and more surprising it came immediately to his summons. The man stood with his eyes open, but he did not see anything around him. The giant had his eyes screwed shut and looked as if he were straining to lift a mountain rather than sitting on the ground.

The ground, the trees and wildlife seemed unchanged to Orrin. In the beginning, he thought there was nothing happening. He was sadly mistaken. The world around them, Orrin included changed. There was new life everywhere. The world was literally bending to the human's will. He was reshaping it as the giant thought it should be. The great Phoenix sat on the man's forearm and looked at him with not contempt but something that looked to Orrin to be pride.

Orrin had seen more than enough to know he was over matched by this little company of heroes, and that was minus Mickalean and the Red. The elf mage opened a portal and slipped away.

Elsewhere, in the Keep of his own creations T'relth was a happy black dragon. He had just returned from his meeting with the powerful mage, an elf named Orrin. No introduction was needed. Thurv and Rolf had been in the elf's home not long ago. Even Malfeezanz knew of this and had some minor business with him through agents, but never in person. Orrin was well known for paying well for knowledge, he was also well known for painful reminders that cheating him was a death sentence. Therefore, Mal wisely stayed away from direct contact with the wily elf, because Mal cheated everybody.

"Did he take the bait master?" Rolf asked.

"Of-course he did you idiot bootlicker" Thurv blurted "do you think T'relth would be in a good mood if he had not. How have you survived all these years, you're not much of a thinker are you, and they call me a mindless monster".

"Boys don't fight, daddy is home and it all went well as Thurv pointed out" the dragon turned human offered to calm the moment down.

"So what now boss" Mal asked.

The black dragon did not answer right away, although he knew the answer already. It was obvious to all except Mal that T'relth had a used for the devious goblin king, and it was not a good or generous use, likely the little monster was going to perish.

"If Orrin fails against the human, and he will because the Red protects him. You dear Malfeezanz will have the privilege of bringing the human to me to be killed" T'relth said evenly.

"Good luck with that Mal" Rolf chuckled.

"Indeed his time has truly come" Thurv said as a follow up.

"Why not send Thurv or Rolf after him, no doubt their great courage will pull them through the task," Mal said cleverly.

"A good argument Mal, but sadly I need you to do it, for these two and others will be setting traps for the little helper following the human around" T'relth stated.

"Very well master; when do you want me to bring him here. I am sure you want to coordinate your attacks and defense for maximum effect" Mal asked.

"Your good judgment and understanding of the situation makes me grieve the necessity of sending you after the human. You have been a fine student for me Malfeezanz. I had thought it a poor idea when I took you on to teach you the ways of magic, I was happy to be in error" the black dragon said.

"I will give Orrin one day to complete his task and fail then you will lure the man here so I can deal with him personally" T'relth said.

"May I ask; what if the elf mage succeeds master" Mal asked?

"I seriously doubt it, the odds are very much against the completion of the task for Orrin, who is old and arrogant, not to mention I set him up to fail" T'relth explain while he laughed deeply.

DRAGON & FIRE TALE

CHAPTER 26: ALONG CAME A DRAGON.

In a clearing ahead of Shaun and company was a very small blue gold dragon name Tag. She was young and really playful and had an amazing secret. Tag had watched from a distance the battles between the goblins and Shaun's group. She saw the giant come up and start some shit, then get his big ass whipped like a naughty child. She watched Shaun and the Phoenix heal the land. However, all of this was small tatters compared to the pain Tag could feel in Shaun over his wife murder. There would be serious hell to pay soon.

The blue dragon watched Orrin spying on the Red, the leprechaun and the Were-fox. Strange new creatures that were a human and angel hybrid sat upon the giant's shoulders, Tag was curious about them. They were so very elegant and beautiful, she was enchanted with them.

Shaun walked into a clearing and there sitting on a rock was a blue dragon with a gold spine and wing tips. It's eyes were gold like it's back and it was smiling at Shaun. The Phoenix started forward and it pulled up short because the Red was already in the blue dragon's face.

"ROOOOOOAAAAR" the Red shook the ground with the intensity of his bellow.

"Oh, Piss off old bean" Tag said with a smile.

The Red stopped his mighty below and looked straight at Tag at extremely close proximity. The tiny blue dragon only smiled as if the mighty king of all dragons was just another fellow that she had just been introduced to.

"Who are you, and what do you want" the Red asked in angry voice.

"I am Tag, the tiny. I do not have to tell you that, tiny I mean. I offer no threat or assault. However, Red I will accept none either" Tag answered honestly.

"Why are you so small if you're a dragon" Shaun asked?

"Alas, I am a pigmy dragon. I will not grow larger than my current size. Moreover, though I am very young by dragon standards, I am very clever and an excellent ally" Tag said in reply.

The group looked over Tag for a while and they were thinking what in the world this mini dragon could possibly be here for. Was she there to offer them harm, betrayal or death. Most of the adventures, including the angels knew enough to beware of strangers or easy gifts.

The small blue dragon, which was no larger than a horse seemed to be very confident. Not over confident mind you, just confident. He sat smiling at the group, was not intimidated by the Red at all, and the Phoenix did not seem to be bothered either. That made everyone a little leery of her. It was Micky who finally approached Tag. The mighty yet tiny leprechaun marched up and looked right in Tag's face. They spent a few moments sizing each other up.

"So laddieie why are ye here now in er path, are you er friend or enemy. If you lie I weel know and I will react in the appropriate wee" Micky told Tag.

"You are a mighty foe Patrick Savage Mickalean and I do not desire you as an enemy" Tag said. "Mind you lil fella, I am in no way afraid of any of you separately or together".

"Braggart, boaster, liar" The Red growled!

What happened next startled even the Red. The eyes of the little dragon began to cloud and swirl inside his eyes. The next thing all of the company knew they were watching the battle between Shaun and Brick, but from Tag's perspective, which included the things they did not see for themselves the first time around. The one that stood out for everyone was Orrin.

"Orrin still lives, Jesus, Mary and Joseph, I thought I killed that pest the last time we met" Micky said. "Guess, I better finish the job this time".

"Rat bastard son of a bitch, I thought I killed him as well," Shaun gargled out in anger.

"Calm your heart Shaun, Orrin is an elf mage and as such is nearly impossible to kill. He is in-fact likely the most powerful of his kin, and that makes him extremely dangerous. He has only one weakness that is know of, his yearning for knowledge. He would sale his soul for the right knowledge," Argast said in fact.

"Well yes, at any rate, I believe he was here to kill him (she points at Shaun with his tail) but he could not while the Phoenix was merged with the man. I would go farther and say that the elf was sent by another who wants you dead much worse that the elf, who would gain nothing from your death" Tag said.

"How do you figure in mate" Asked Trevor, who was still in poor condition after his ordeal?

The tiny blue gold dragon smiled at Trevor and winked at him as if that was the correct question at the correct time.

"I have decided to take a more active role in the happenings of man, such as the Red has. I believe that this man in particular is more important to this world than any of us. Therefore, I will intervene in the affairs that guide his destiny to make sure that ruination and damnation are not visited on all of our heads" Tag said.

"That is very benevolent of you, but I think there is more laddie" Mick said with a serious chuckle.

Tag made a serious face and narrowed her golden orbs, as if he were trying to find the right way to explain or avoid the explanation that either way would expose him to unpleasantries.

"Gentlemen, I am not a lad for the first thing as the Red well knows. Second, the Black known as T'relth is making all dragons look bad and that cannot be allowed if we are to get along with humanity. Man is already scared to death of dragon kind and the last thing we need is a dragon slayer war as were waged in the past" Tag explained.

"What can such a tiny dragon maiden do to stop the Black" Fox inquired in a suspicious tone?

The blue golden dragon opened her mind and captured all of them at once. She held them immobile for several minutes, and then released them. Fox took exception to being toyed with and attacked.

Tag let her come in hot and dangerous, then snapped her tail out and caught fox in her tail and held on to her firmly. Fox tried to transform but found she could not. Tag saw this revelation and put Fox down.

"I have many talents Goddess of the Wilderness; you just experienced two of them. I can block magic use while in contact with a person and I can move fast than any creature" Tag said without any hint of pomp or pride. She was merely stating factoids.

Fox was angry but she saw the truth of the situation and did not renew her aggression toward Tag. She looked at Micky, the

Red and Shaun as if to say it was up to them as the more powerful members of the troupe. Nevertheless, it was Trevor who put it all into perspective for them.

"Very neatly done darling, you had us all on are bums before we even knew what for. You are true to your words alright, I would stake me life on et" Trevor said in his usual good-natured way. "If you kin stop me lover like that, without hurting her, then your with us, not against".

The rock under Tag exploded suddenly in a violent explosion startling everyone except Shaun.

"However, Lassie, if you mean me girl any harm, any harm at all I will kill ya, count on it" Trevor said with deadly seriousness.

The small blue dragon was just as startled by Trevor's lightning fast attack as the others. She had no indication that he would attack. He closed his mind like a pro, and then punctuated his meaning clearly enough for a goblin to glean it.

Tag must not take any of these heroes lightly, each one of them was a work of art in their own way, but together they were a masterpiece, and dangerous in the extreme.

"Loud and clear hunter" Tag said.

The group made camp at Tag's request while she explained her thoughts and a plan to get their enemies to face them all at once. Hide and seek was not a dragon game of choice, facing a foe straight up was, so once again T'relth was a disgrace to dragon blood. Moreover, the Black was next in all out power level to the Red, which made a plan problematic at best. The Red explained that he and He alone would deal with T'relth without interference of any kind. Nobody argued with him wisely.

Tag turned out to be a wealth of information and constructed plans, complete with secondary options for different scenarios.

Even Fox who was distrustful by nature could feel the rightness about Tag. The tiny female dragon was the first Fox had ever met who was female or a pigmy. Fox had wrongly assumed that dragons were asexual. A sudden burst of laughter made Fox look up. Tag and the Red were both smiling at her. Damn, Fox forgot that dragons are almost always telepathic.

In her mind Fox heard plain as day ("Fox, we are an old and social race. We are as frisky as kittens most of the time among our own kind. It is a rare event when a female dragon is ever seen outside of our holds because they are the greatest treasures a dragon can have, so they are protected above all else" The Red whispered into her mind).

The angels were so interested in Tag that they went as far as to ask Brick if he would pickup Tag so they could get a closer look. They were far too afraid of dragons to go near her without Brick to give them support. Tag knew that, so she jumped into the air and landed beside the angels on Brick's shoulder. She lay down and beckoned to Sera and Liri to come closer and visit with her. Tag later admitted she quite liked it when the blond giant held her in his arms and scratch between her wings or behind her golden horns and spikes.

There was something that Tag did not share and she blocked her mind to keep the Red out of this knowledge. She believed what she knew could change the world one way or the other. Her course was never in question, she must protect the world as best she could, no matter that her kind heart burned with the knowledge she so wanted to share.

Everyday Trevor got stronger than the day before. It was likely because Fox had expressed her love of him and told him that when he was strong enough she would take him into her bed as well as her heart. Therefore, Trevor worked out and ate as well as he could each day as if he had to do so just to live. The fact is that he just wanted Fox with a terrible passion. Luckily for the Irishman she felt the same way, which was a new thing for her a singularly solitary being. She made a no turning back decision about Trevor and offered him her heart. Yes, she knew about his romantic conquests and exploits, none of that mattered. He was hers and she knew it. Fox was not like any woman Trevor had ever known, she had that certain thing, the one thing all other woman before her lacked. She had his heart and interest and not only for sex, but for life. Trevor made the same decision Fox did, if she would have him, than he would give it all to her, heart and soul.

Hours seemed like day to Shaun, his heart burned one only one thing **VENGENCE**. The others knowing how powerful Shaun was and maddening as it was, he seemed to be growing more powerful all the time. He was not a stable boy in any way. He was getting more distant and quiet all the time. To hear Shaun's voice was a rare moment. It seemed only a matter of time before he was too powerful for them to kill or stop, which in Shaun's case were the same thing. A second major problem was the Phoenix; they could not even try to harm Shaun with it around. If they were fool enough to try, all that would remain of them to show the world they had lived would be ashes. Therefore, as you can guess they were very concerned.

"Do you wish me dead so much" Shaun asked out of the blue, without even looking at them.

They all looked at one another, not knowing if the time had come or if Shaun had come to his senses. Even the mighty Argast and god among his kind was cautious of an ill chosen word.

"Why would you ask us this" Red asked

"I can hear all of your thoughts like a radio station, except Tag's. I know that you're scared of me and that you think I might go nova a out of the blue, well, it won't happen. I do not want to hurt the world anymore than Brick does. I would not kill off a new love like the one Trevor and Fox have found, and my dragon friends as well. I am not a monster, if I become one the Phoenix has

179

already agreed to burn me to dust at my request" Shaun said sadly. "It makes me sad that my own companions and so called friends would even think about killing me"?

CHAPTER 27: INSANITY

Sayu and Mara had been walking for several days, when Mara decided enough of this. She put her well-toned arm around Sayu's waist and took to the sky. Sayu had avoided this because she did not know how long Mara could carry her without hurting herself. Sayu had been selfish for more than a thousand years, so her affection and desire to protect Mara off balanced her. Not a feeling she craved. Mara on the other hand was in-tune with the world and had more than enough endurance to make any journey carrying her much-loved friend. Mara and Sayu were so close it seemed unnatural not to be with and do everything together.

"We will arrive at the location of my sisters in an hour, they are no longer moving" Mara said as she flapped her tawny white wings.

"Does that mean they are hurt or dead" Sayu asked.

"No, I would know if any real harm had come to them" Mara answered, with a smile and a soft kiss on the cheek.

Mara miss read Sayu's feels toward her sisters completely. When Sayu asked about them, Mara thought she was asking in concern for them. Sayu was actually hoping they were dead so precious Mara would be all hers. Sayu knew also that was not to be, sooner or later Mara's goddess body and angel heart would bring a man or woman into her bed and heart.

At that time, Sayu will have to let her go. She grieved for the first days when Mara had regained her human form. Sayu was not used to caring for anyone, but now that she did it was painful to think of loosing Mara.

It was just as Mara said it would be. Sayu and Mara literally fell out of the sky into the middle of the adventurer's camp.

Before they knew what happened they were blasted across the camp in a blaze of white-hot fire.

"I am sick of being attacked all the time" Shaun screamed as the very dirt began to burn.

"Oh Shoit, were in the soup now, Shaun has finally lost his mind" Micky yelled.

"Oh My God Mara are you okay" Sera screamed as she ran to the girls who were covered in fire.

"I will allow no more attacks on my person, if you want to fuckin fight bring it" Shaun said as tears ran down his cheeks. He stomped his right foot and a flame shockwave flattened everyone, even the Red.

The scene was a nightmarish hell with everything burning. Brick had jumped down on his hands and knees in front of the angels to keep the blast from killing his loved ones. Brick looked back over his shoulder and slammed his fist into the ground; the result was a huge rock hit Shaun in the chest right out of the ground and knocked him back.

There was a haze of movements as Fox grabbed Trevor and tossed him none too gently into Micky's barrier. Micky had placed a protective barrier around the girls, Trevor and Tag in a flash of movement.

"Calm yourself Shaun" the Red said softly yet still loud because he was a dragon.

Fox and Brick took another tact, they attack will a fever like neither had ever known before. They had a common purpose, to protect those they loved, so fear and pain were unknown to them. Shaun did not see them coming since Brick flattened him.

Both combatants got within a tight foot of Shaun when the

world went mad.

Brilliant purple lightning hit Shaun from every angle. His skin burned and his muscles shriveled, yet he did not cry out in pain. Shaun was dying and from the looks, he did not give a shit. That hopelessness made him too dangerous to live. The smell of burnt flesh and singed hair permeated the air and ground. To Fox's horror the corpse that was Shaun got up from the ground; he had blood coming out of his eyes, mouth, ears and the many open burning wounds. He smiled and spit blood on the ground. He turned and looked in the direction of the camp. He had finally snapped; Shaun was insane.

"Now that is what I am talking about" Shaun said in a nigh indiscernible voice.

The burning man waved his hand and anything in the line his hand took was turned to ashes, except, the purple crackling energy ball in front of him. When the purple haze dissipated a once gorgeous woman with a burnt face and bare breasts was standing there with a wild insane visage to rival Shaun's. Her long black was moving around like Medusa's only it was being moved by the raw energy coming from her.

"YOU KILLED MARA" she screamed.

The purple whiplash hit Shaun so hard that his left arm was nearly ripped from his shoulder. The second and third did an equal amount of damage, still Shaun did nothing. He stood there and accepted each devastating blow as if it were a gentle breeze and not a life-ending blow.

"Say something you bastard, I am Sayu the greatest sorcerer that ever lived and you life is forfeit. Still, I want to know the name to have put on your head stone, you less than nothing" Sayu growled at Shaun.

"HAHAHAHAHAHAHAHAHAHAHAHAHA" Shaun's insane

laughter actually scared everyone who heard it. Even Sayu was unhinged.

The man who was torn asunder put his hands together as if he were about to pray and smiled with his burning eyes closed. He suddenly opened his eyes and parted his hands about ten inches apart. Between his hands was a tiny sun, it pulsed with life and the heat could be felt by all. Shaun opened his hands palms out toward Sayu and his launched the sun at her. For all the sorcerer's powers, she would have been atomized if the sun had reached her. At the last possible moment Tag jumped in the sun's path eyes glowing like golden pulsars and she deflected the sun off to the northwest. The canyon that resulted from the sun was a thousand feet deep and five hundred miles long.

"Very good team work" Shaun said calmly.

Once again Shaun closed his eyes, but this time he put his hands out to his sides and power danced from hand to hand across his body.

"MY MAKER" The Red said. "I know this magic it is not fire based, we are without hope if I am correct there is no defense, and alas we are dead".

Shaun was about to end a large part of the world in one toss of the bones. He meant to kill his pain and misery by wiping his perceived enemy.

The Phoenix dropped down into Shaun's line of sight and opened it's mouth letting go of a voiceless scream. However it was not voiceless to Shaun, the energy and magic was instantly gone. Sayu had witnessed this and was about to attack when the Phoenix wheeled on her and a jet of living fire reach out and stopped just short of her face. It was a clear warning not to proceed or interfere in any way. Sayu was old and very powerful, but even she knew how futile it would be to oppose a Phoenix. It was a death sentence if you tried.

Sayu walked up to Shaun with her hands opened in peace to show the Phoenix she meant no harm and she had intended to looked at him with scorn, but when she approached she was filled not with anger. Sayu looked at Shaun sitting there and her heart hurt and she was filled with pity.

Shaun called out to the Phoenix. It came to him. Shaun whispered something in private to the firebird and began to walk over to where Mara lay upon the ground unconscious. Shaun took a deep breath and knelt by her; he leaned over her and kissed her so gently on the lips. Mara's whole body glowed from within for a moment and then faded. Shaun got up and walked up to Sayu, put his arms around her waist pulled her into his arms and kissed her just as softly on the lips. Sayu wanted to resist but she could feel the powerful magic in this sad man and decide she was lucky to just have lived through facing off with him in a combat situation. He was so far beyond her powers that she almost forgot that he was kissing her, until she realized her arms were wrapped around him. She was kissing him passionately back to her surprise. Sayu had never known passion like this before; she was a selfish woman, only Mara had touched her heart in her completely long life. Now she felt drawn to this man and Mara as well, strange the course that life takes she thought. Shaun stepped back and looked into Sayu's beautiful face completely restored. He ran his hand over her face and smiled.

"I'm sorry" Shaun said and began to walk away.

Mara got up and she was completely healed with no sign of any damage, as if it had no occurred. Sayu ran to her and they embraced. Sera and Liri also hugged them both. Sayu realized that she cared for the other angels as well as Mara, strange how I am changing.

"Good lord there are four of them dolls" Trevor said with a chuckle. He turned to Fox and smiled at her, all of her natural jealousy melted away in the love he sent her. She smiled back.

The dragons were off to the side by themselves conversing about something private. Micky was looking hard at Sayu, she had not noticed him before, but now that she had, Sayu's breath caught in her throat.

"MICKALEAN" She said in a loud breathless voice.

Sayu stepped forward and bowed low to the tiny fellow with steely eyes. Micky was not looking kindly on Sayu at all, actually he look very upset.

"She has changed tiny man" Mara said sweetly.

"Er, does that be a fact lass" Micky said quizzically.

"Sayu released us from the hell that was our harpy bodies and made us this" Mara said then swept her hands down her body.

"Yes ye are a beauty miss, but no doubt it were Sayu who did the black deed of turning you into a harpy in the first case" Micky replied wisely.

"Sera and I were actually made or remade by Mara not Sayu" Liri said. "Sayu does not want us around. Mara as the senior sister told us to go with our giant love Brick. She knew he would need our protection soon and thus we could not stay with her when we are needed to save a friend".

The sorcerer looked at Liri in a new light, the girl was so lovely and gentle, Sayu had a wave of guilt slam into her as if she were hit by a giant. Sayu had tears on her cheeks before she knew they were falling. Sera came and held her close and consoled her. Liri and Mara barred Micky from approaching Sayu. Both of their beautiful eyes were radiating power, Mara's pale blue-green and Sera's blue. There was no mistaking their stance, they were going to protect Sayu with their lives and not because Sayu ordered it but because they loved her. Micky decided to

186

hold his judgment of Sayu for the time being. He smiled at the angels and bowed to them.

"Ok ladies, I weel take yer werd for it, for now" Micky said.

Mara watched Shaun march off into the woods, every step he took left new plant life growing. That man was healing the damage he had done, but he could not heal his own heart, how sad.

The red haired angel made to follow Shaun when Tag stopped her.

"Think twice little one; that man is not to be messed with. His pain runs very deep, so before you disturb him be sure you are willing to pay the price of that choice" Tag lectured.

"I appreciated your concern for my person but I care only for others. Right now that man needs me and I will go help heal his heart" Mara said as Sayu walked up to hold her hand.

The two girls walked into the woods after Shaun. A half an hour later they came to a small lake where Shaun was sitting on a rock crying. Mara said nothing when she looked at Sayu. She led the sorcerer to Shaun, where she knelt down and put her head on his shoulder and her free right arm around his waist. Sayu did the same on the left side. The three of them sat there for hours just holding each other. When Shaun kissed Mara on the head, and then did the same to Sayu; he felt he was ready to speak to them at that point; feeling himself calm enough to tell the story of his life and why he was here now. They both cried, never had Sayu felt such anguish and pain, So great was Shaun's love for Ayla that he would destroy the world to repay her loss. Mara had her head on Shaun's thigh; because she was weak from crying so hard. Mara also wanted to know a love this great for herself.

"I am tired and it is dark you should go back to the others and sleep. The Red will protect you from any harm" Shaun said kindly.

"No, I will stay and hold you through the night; you must not be alone anymore, ever. I promise to stay by your side as long as I live" Mara said.

Sayu's shock face at this pledge was replaced by admiration and love. "I would know the comfort of your body this night and all the nights of you life Shaun. I pledge to you all my power and as much of my heart as I can give as I am not good at giving. I am very good at pleasure though Shaun with the sad eyes" Sayu said.

"Ok, if you must, but I am not good company" Shaun said. "I can't have you sleeping out here unprotected".

Fire jumped from Shaun's hands and dance around the clearing, it turned the sand to glass and the glass to a small structure. It was of the most spectacular colors. More, it was pulsing and warm to the touch. Shaun opened the door and walked inside. The girls followed him and were surprised to find the inside furnished. There was a water basin on a wooden stump like table. There a bed of soft woven fibers that Shaun sat on. You could see out clearly but not in.

"We are completely secure in here, only my Phoenix brother could enter without my permission" Shaun said.

The angel Mara spread her wings and wrapped them around Shaun. She kissed him on the lips softly, then she stood folded her wings away and was smooth backed again. Shaun got up and ran his hand over her back. She Smiled at him, placed a hand on his chest began to heal him but the effort was too great.

"Poor child, I am so sorry. I can heal my own body quite easily" Shaun said. He closed his eyes and burst into flame for an instant only, when the flames died he was young and whole again without any scars.

"Can you teach me that trick love" Sayu said. She was lying on the bed nude, patting the bed beside her.

Mara took off her cloth and crawled on to the bed beside her lovely companion. Mara stopped and took Shaun's hand and pulled him on to the bed. When he was flat on his back, they fell on to him with a gentle loving touch and kisses. Somewhere late that night Shaun gave in and they become lovers. The sun would rise before they finally stopped to rest. It was the first decent sleep he had had since Ayla died.

The trios came back in the late morning to the main camp. Mara and Sayu were holding hands following Shaun up the trial. Even Shaun looked marginally happy when he stopped and looked at Trevor. The adventurer gave Shaun the thumbs up. Micky was in a three way discussion with dragons.

Shaun cleared his throat and made an announcement.

"I suggest you make all make your peace with God, make love, eat a good meal, sleep as much as you can. On the morning of two days from now; I am going after the goblin king who killed my wife, and the elf mage who came to kill me and the dragon who sent them both after me" Shaun said without malice. It was merely a fact he stated.

DRAGON & FIRE TALE

CHAPTER 28: THE FINAL ANSWER

In the small hours of the morning Malfeezanz crept into the camp of the Red expecting to enter undetected. Mal was no fool, he had lived through many years as the king of goblins and that is no small task. Goblins are tough and mean, sometimes gullible but not stupid, so the king must be smarter and meaner just to live.

Many eyes watched the wily goblin walk so softly to avoid making any sounds with a goblin short sword in his grey-scarred knuckles. Poor fool did not expect that he would be invited into a trap, but he was.

There was a blur of motion off to the right, flowed by an explosion and the sword was harshly knocked out of Mal's hand. The goblin tried to toss up a magic barrier but he suddenly was pinned to the ground by the biggest hand he had ever seen. Then there were these burning eyes looking down at him, and the goblin knew his days were gone, all his checks were cashed, all debts, markers were now due.

"Bring him" The burning eyes said.

Mal was tied up in a way that would allow him to escape back to T'relth when the time was right. It was a complicated trap, but a thorough one. The goblin king was sure that it was a trap as well, but he played along. Mal valued his own life more than he feared the dragon he called master. T'relth should have known this.

"Well now lad where is yer master" Micky asked?

"Why should I say anything I am dead already" Mal snapped.

"Simple lackey, we don't want you, we want your boss, and the big worm T'relth" Tag said.

"You're a mere child compared to the Black, what could you do midget" Mal barked?

"She is not the Black's foe I am" Bellowed Argast, shaking the ground.

"Look guys, the Black is not alone, he has trolls and my vast goblin armies, and Rolf to help him fight you, so completely out numbered are you that there is no hope" Mal said.

Three of the most beautiful women Mal had ever seen walked out of the dark. They all had wings and blue eyes. To the lecherous goblin, they were fresh meat to be raped and played with. He soon learned not to underestimate a woman again. He still was sore from where Ayla cut his throat. If he had told Shaun Ayla was alive, Mal might have been let go, but the goblin never thought of it, because he is a goblin and the truth is odd to them.

The angel with brown hair and butterfly wings knelt and slapped Mal hard in the face.

"That was for all the ladies you killed monster" Sera said.

"Set him free and let us have him" Mara said as she let lightning dance from one hand to the other.

The goblin was afraid; these girls were magic users and not run of the mill either. They were heavy hitters; Mal started thinking that T'relth was in for a few surprises. The last member of the group was a shy little one and she had glowing blue eyes and she touched the other two then touched Mal. She entered his mind like a battering ram; she ripped through his memories at will. Liri gathered all the information she thought she needed and let Mal go.

"He sent you to die Malfeezanz, you are cannon fodder" Liri said over her shoulder as she walked away.

"You know he is the one who killed Shaun's wife right" Liri said to Sayu who was not in the light so Mal didn't know she was there?

"Yes, I know, but Shaun doesn't so let's keep it quiet about it for now" Sayu said.

"Are you afraid Shaun will blow the plans, or do you care about him" Liri asked Sayu?

(Smile) "Strangely, I find that I have strong feelings for him. He is the first man or woman that I have let near me who is more powerful than myself, I find that it turns me on to be dominated, although he is of gentle heart" Sayu said.

Brick and Shaun stayed back and watched for other goblins or werewolves or whatever that would likely be jumping out at them when they were not ready. The Red was sure that T'relth would not send just this fool to attack Shaun, without back up. Strangely, that is exactly what he did, knowing full well Mal could not win.

"I think we should let him slip away soon while it is still dark, that way they wont be sure from where we will be coming from" Trevor said.

"Agreed. Trevor are you going to be alright when the fighting starts, not to be an ass but you a strict human" Shaun said?

"I will put a bind around him, what that does is, it make Trevor impossible to shoot, stab, or cut with any kind of weapon. However, magic can still be used so kill anyone who is casting at you quickly" The Red offered.

"Good Show Red, I will take the extra armor and I promise to keep the goblins out of yer faces" Trevor said with his usual smile.

"I will seek out the wolf and put his dick in the dirt as Trevor says" Fox chuckled "No matter what do not interfere Trevor, even if I look to be losing. Promise me boy or no more loving".

"OIY, I promised gal, sheez calm down" Trevor laughed as he put his powerful arm around Fox's waist.

The moment the adventurers turned their backs on Mal to act as if they were planning the goblin slipped out of his bonds and snapped open a portal and jumped into the out and was gone. It anyone was watching the companions in the dark they would have seen a complete set of smiles and teeth showing.

"So It begins. It has been a pleasure meeting you people and other folks as well (Shaun put his hand on Argast front knee), some of us may not live through what is coming" Shaun said,

"I for one will not stop until we have put that evil scum to heel" Tag added.

"Watch your back youngling, I am fond of your golden eyes. If we should parish this day, I would have you know my name. I am Argast" The great red dragon said softly so only Tag could hear. Her scales and Golden spine seemed to glow, which was likely her form of blushing.

The next moment was one of the most amazing sights anyone had ever seen. Brick began to shrink until he was a mere seven feet tall, down from 30 foot tall. He walked over to Liri and picked her up in his massively muscled arms and kissed her passionately. He stopped for a moment and reached out for Sera. She came to his open arm, he scooped her up.

Brick said, "I need both of my loved ones to know of my

affection before I spend my life in battle. I love you both. Brick kissed Sera just as passionately as he had Liri.

"I had thought it was only Liri that you wanted, I never hoped to share your love" Sera said with tears on her cheeks. She put her head on Brick's shoulder, as did Liri and they stayed that way. It seemed that they did not want to be parted now that they had openly confessed love.

"We will be helpful to you in battle Brick, we have our own special powers that will make us useful to you" Liri said as she looked at Mara, who smiled.

"Ready yourselves" Argast said as he ripped open the portal Mal had taken.

The portal opened and they jumped out ready for battle but there were no armies waiting only a single person was there. An elf mage.

"Hold, I would speak with you openly without combat" Orrin said.

"Speak" Argast bellowed, causing Orrin to blanch.

"I was set up to die when T'relth sent me after him. (He pointed at Shaun). I was not told about you or Mickalean, thus I did not try to follow through. I like not treachery. I offer you safe passage to T'relth's Keep in repayment for his deeds, then my debt is paid" Orrin explained.

"Agreed" Shaun said.

"A moment lad if ye pleezes, I am not for trustin this one, him I knows, and he is not our friend" Micky said.

Orrin turn and looked hard at Micky, who happily returned his stare. Argast thought they would go to open warfare at any moment, but it did not happen.

"I understand that Mick, but I want root not the cause of our troubles and that is a black dragon" Shaun said.

"Very weel, but the elf goes through feerst, just to make sure that we don't get boned" Micky said with a smile, his green eyes ablaze.

The elf opened the portal and went in, the group poured in behind him, with Argast going first against Shaun's wishes. Brick went third, with his angels on his once again 30ft high shoulders.

The Keep was getting ready when Mal came to the barrier and rang the attention bell. Rolf let him in with a cuff on the shoulder. They went directly to T'relth's meeting chamber, where a war counsel was in session. Mal walked in and bowed to the dragon. Thurv looked at Mal and behind him as well.

"Empty handed Mal, there is a surprise" Thurv said with a snicker.

"Be still Troll. What has happened" T'relth said?

The entire tales was laid out for the Black, and he listened without interruption to all of it. Then he surprised all of the gathered forces by smiling. To say the assembled were confused would be an understatement. Mal thought he was to be killed; T'relth knew this and put that notion to rest.

"I asked you to bring them to me; I never said you must die to complete the task. You are too valuable to kill of a trivial missed opportunity" The dragon explained.

"We don't need him master" Rolf said.

"Really and who will lead the goblin armies, you" Mal said?

"Yes" Rolf growled.

196

"No you fool, goblins will not follow another creature except a dragon and I have no time to see to minor details" T'relth said in a final tone.

"Guess I better do it then, and save Rolf from the slaughter" Mal said in a snide way.

"Anytime you want to try me dirt-bag be my guest, no goblin could ever take a wolf" Rolf roared and lunged at Malfeezanz.

The black dragon clothes lined him.

"Imbecile, you may be able to take up to ten goblins, but how about a hundred or a thousand? You would be dead in minutes at the most" T'relth hissed at Rolf!

Thurv grabbed Rolf by the back of his neck and Mal and shook they like rag dolls and then snarled in their faces.

"No more horseshit you two or I'll kill ya myself and eat you" Thurv spit into their faces.

The meeting came back to order and T'relth outlined his plans for crushing his foe, namely the Red. He indicated that they others were to kill all of the allies as they could. Once T'relth takes care of the Red; he will wipe the rest out in conclusion. Rolf was not happy at being push into a minor role, he always felt like a strong fighter, so he want to take the lead into battle. T'relth told him no, first the goblins would advance and weaken the Red's company and divide them, that way each could be eliminated separately.

The elf mage Orrin was good to his word, he took them directly to the Keep as agreed, and then he simply back away and disappeared. The Red took a defensive posture and looked around in the new light of the coming day. Once all of the adventurers were through the portal it closed with a slight flash.

The group spread out and started looking over the land to see where the best places to attack and defend were. Shaun was going to turn all fire but the Red and Tag ask him to hold off. Brick took a knee behind some trees.

"Hey, they don't know we are here yet, we came in before they were ready for us" He said.

"I concur, we have them by surprise. I do not smell or sense any goblins, trolls or wolves either" Fox said.

It was impossible to hide from Fox she was the best hunter killer in the world.

"I da not sense magic wards either lads, but this is a dragon's territory, so maybe Ms. Tag could sweep the area fer us" Micky said?

"No need master Micky, your correct there is no magic at work here" Tag assured him.

Fox began her full transformation to the Were-Fox in all her glory, when she stopped and asked Trevor a question.

"What is that" Fox asked?

Trevor had brought a shotgun, a P90, two Glock automags, six big knives, and a case. Trevor slung the shotgun across his shoulders and strapped the P90 to his belly. He reached down and opened the case and took out a huge mech-rifle.

"This lil babe is my BFG" He said with a chuckle. He reached down and put a clip into the rifle and slide the slide and let it click. Trevor put the other two clips in his vest.

"Three clips will not be enough lover" Fox said.
198

"Not true Fox, each one of these clips contains ten thousand miniature aluminum BB's, that are 1/10 size of the ones used in a BB gun. They are electrically charged and shot out at light speed, when they hit they explode because of the speed they are going" Trevor beamed.

"Nice weapon, what does BFG" Fox asked

(Sly Laugh) "Big Fucking Gun" Trevor explained.

"Of-course; that makes sense" Fox said, kissed Trevor and finished changing.

The entire group began to make their way to the Keep. They were half way there when a goblin guard on the wall screamed that they were under siege, all hell broke out. Fireballs filled the air. Brick stepped forward and just swatted them harmlessly aside. Shaun thought turnabout is fair play, so he filled the air with flames that slammed into an invisible barrier.

"What do wee have er" Micky said?

"I can break it no problem" Shaun said.

"No, that is not breakable. The world would be destroyed before the barrier broke. It is a fine example of the famed Black dragon barrier" Argast said.

The red dragon took to wing and started bellowing insults at the keep. He flew around and around the barrier, measuring it, insults fall down from above. It would appear that T'relth had heard enough and called out to his greatest foe.

"Let us break up into single combats, and test our metal against yours Red" T'relth offered. "Your word of honor you will not attack if I drop the barrier"?

Mal ran to the dragon all-frantic.

"Master you can't, he will kill us all. You can not trust him to keep his word" Mal screamed.

The Black smacked Mal and knocked him rolling end over end. Mal sat up and the Black was glaring at him.

"He is not you or I, Mal. He has an honor that is the envy of all; his word is not breakable once given. You are nobody to question my judgment or the Red's honor Goblin" T'relth snarled.

"Despite your lowlife lackeys insults, we agree to your terms. Winner take all, correct" Argast replied

"So let it be done then" T'relth answered.

The barrier dropped and so did both gates. Goblins by the tens ran out both gates heading for the valley off to the side of the Keep. Argast looked at Trevor, who gave a quick nod and took off after the goblins into the valley. He smacked Fox on her furry muscular butt on the way by. She growled at him and smiled.

A huge figure with a spiked club walked out the main gate. He was massive, 15 feet tall at-least and fifteen hundred pounds if an ounce. The look on his face was priceless when he saw Brick standing there looking at him. Brick took one-step forward and said only one word to his friends.

"Mine"

Thurv walked of the hill just above the Keep on the right and waited for Brick to come to him. Brick was way bigger than the troll, yet the troll did not seem concerned. That made Liri and Sera who sat on his shoulders worry. Brick walked up to Thurv and stunned everyone.

"Well old friend, how are you. Am I to assume you have thrown

in with the worm" Brick asked as he shook Thurv's hand?

"Yep, for better or worse buddy, I am in it to win it. So, I take it you are to be my opponent, that works for me, just like old times" Thurv said as he stepped back a pace.

"Afraid so Bud, I will take great pleasure in whipping your ass" Brick said with a smile.

Shaun and Tag were watching this exchange baffled as to what was going on. The troll and giant had history to be sure. What put Shaun off was that they didn't seem serious about that combat. He was deadly wrong about that.

"Hey Brick can I ask for a boon" Thurv said?

"Why not, call it professional courtesy" Brick said.

"Good, can we not fight eye to eye Brick; you are twice my size after all" Thurv said.

Shaun saw the logic and knew that Brick would grant the request since it was single combat. The troll no doubt would be cheating. Brick dropped his size until he was 16 feet in height.

"Shall we begin, and what about these two" Thurv said pointing to Sera and Liri.

"They are with me, I could not get rid of them even if I wanted to" Brick stated.

The blow from the club the troll carried hit Brick right in the face, just as Sera back-flipped off Brick's shoulder into the air above his head pulling Liri up with her. Brick took a step to the side to balance himself and hit the troll squarely on top of his head. The troll found that he had been driven into the ground two feet from the heft of the impact like a lawn dart. Brick ripped the club out of Thurv's hands and bitch slapped him with his left

DRAGON & FIRE TALE

hand. Brick tossed the club into the forest beyond, it landed on some goblins sending them to their maker.

"Children should not play with dangerous toys" Brick said.

"You Muther F..."Thurv began to say as he caught a wicked right hook.

"Tut tut, troll, no foul language" Brick chuckled.

The troll hit the ground like a bull elephant dropped out of an airplane from ten thousand feet. He was spitting out teeth when he stood up and snarled. Thurv was no longer playing battle tag with Brick, now he wanted to kill him. The troll extended his claw-like fingernails and raked across Brick's chest, which tore his shirt right off. There was a thin line across Brick's chest but nothing more. If it had not been Brick that the troll racked, another being would have been sliced in half.

"Ouch... no, just kidding" Brick said.

"SCREEEEEEECH"!!!

This time the giant went to his knees. His skin was invincible but his ears were not. The troll used his special ability as a weapon against his old friend. Brick tried to gain his feet again, but Thurv let another blast go and toppled Brick.

The troll should have been paying better attention to the angels above his head. Sera and Liri were holding hands and they were covered in the blue light that matched their eye color. They looked at Thurv as he pulled back his head drawing in a mighty breath. The troll finally saw them at the last moment and remembered that they were with Brick. It was way too late to save himself.

"YOU TRIED TO KILL OUR BRICK" they said in one singing voice.

A bolt of pure blue light shot straight down Thurv's throat. However it was not just light, no it was magic. The angels could shape the magic by their will. This light was the light of un-making, what they unmade was the trolls throat muscles and by default his ability to screech. Thus, no more weapon.

The cocky troll had thought he had Brick just where he wanted him, he screeched and the giant moaned, he kicked Brick and the giant coughed as if his ribs were broken. It would have been sad if it were not so funny from where Shaun and Tag were. Remember for a second that the giant Brick was invincible to physical harm. All the time Thurv was putting the boot to Brick the angels Sera and Liri were healing their lover's eardrums. When their work was done Brick just stood up, while he was on his knees he grew 6 feet.

"How did you overcome my yell" Thurv said, then gave a hard screech.

The handsome giant just looked down, but no longer did he smile. He made the transition to righteous indignation. The troll looked up and understood his time had come; he had pushed his luck beyond good measure. Thurv's usual good judgment had been left behind when he thought he had Brick killed, therefore the absence of a credible back up plan cost him not only the contest this time but his life. Brick was serious and Thurv had seen him serious only once before and the damage the mad giant did was legendary.

"Good bye Thurv" Brick said calmly.

"It has been a gas Brick, shake for old time sake" said the troll, holding out his hand.

To everyone's surprise Brick reached forward and shook the proffered hand. Thurv smiled and patted Brick on the arm. A moment later, they stepped apart. Thurv began to circle, but Brick moved faster than a humming bird. He snatch the troll king by the nape of his neck, hoisted him over his head. Brick grabbed the back of Thurv's right leg and bent the troll in half. Thurv's head was touching his butt. There was a thunderclap when the troll's massive spine gave way. The giant slammed the troll into the ground until you could no longer tell what they creature was when he started the beating. So passed Thurv the greatest of all the troll kings.

The battle for the valley went poorly for the goblins, which saw only the human and did not count of his mega-rifle and the exploding rounds.

"Come to papa boys" Trevor sang to them.

Goblin arrows bounce off the magic barrier placed by Argast around Trevor, as did the spears. However, in close quarter combat the goblins were doing better. No matter how fast Trevor shot, the goblins just climbed on their own dead to get at him. Somehow they got the rifle out of Trevor's hands, thus they thought him beaten. Wrong answer.

"Veery good lads, colm taste me steel" Trevor said pulling two massive Bowie knives.

There were thousands of goblins when the battle started, only a few hundred were left before Trevor lost his rifle. One hour later the savage human berserker had cut the number to ten. Never, had a goblin seen a man fight with such zeal.

"Human, hold a moment" Said Malfeezanz. "You are without peer among your race. When you finally die I shall name you Trevor of the thousand cuts, for surely you have had that many and still you fight".

"Yeel naw down me, ya harses arse, I got enuff in me to finish'r op" Trevor said as bleed seeped through his teeth.

The goblin king raised his hand began to chant a spell; he

made only a few syllables before he was on his knees as Shaun's feet. The goblin's throat was ripped open. Trevor looked shocked.

"My apologies Trevor you have done very well today without any help, but this one was special" Shaun said.

"We didn't think you knew who he was" Trevor gargled up.

"I knew, I always knew, I just waited until the right time my friend. That time is here and now" Shaun snarled as he tossed the goblin in the dirt.

The goblin went to healing himself as he bounced. He was on his feet and about run when Shaun slammed a fist into his kidneys, and Mal was on the ground again. Mal rolled over in terror.

"WAIT YER WIFE IS NOT DEAD, T'RELTH HAS HER IN THE KEEP...I SWEAR" Mal screamed.

"Riiiight" Shaun said.

Flames licked out between Shaun's teeth, much like a dragon's before the breath of fire. Shaun took no deep breathe, no he just opened his mouth and incinerated Malfeezanz right there on the ground where he was cringing. Therefore, this day the smartest cross species goblin in history had made one too few calculations, and his account was settled forever.

When their king paid the price for his mistakes, all the living goblins came forward, took a knee and bowed to Shaun. They tossed their weapons on the ground at his feet.

"We will fight no more, we follow only our king and you have killed him. You may kill us or let us go, as the victor" a giant goblin said.

"Stand up big spokes goblin" Shaun said

The big goblin did as he was bid. He was taller than Shaun. Shaun reached down and picked the best weapon up. It was the jeweled sword of Malfeezanz. He held it to the goblins throat. The goblin did not move, for goblins fear not death.

"I name you King Big shoulders of all goblins, and I give you Mal's sword. Swear loyalty to me and that you will attack no humans unprovoked and you may go free" Shaun said.

"I lead my own way as long as I swear to your service if you call on me" Big S said?

"Yes that is so" Shaun answered.

"Done, you have my word, when you call all goblins will come to your summons" Big stated. He took the sword from Shaun and departed.

When the goblins were just out of sight Trevor dropped to the ground. Shaun leaned over him and the Pure Flame Of the Inferno was once again used on Trevor to fix and preserve his valuable life.

"Why not wipe them out, why king the big one" Trevor spit out in pain.

"We don't kill for the hell of it, we are not monsters, and the big dude will keep the others at bay. The strongest goblin rules the tribe that is their way, their law" Shaun explained.

"Where is Fox lad" Trevor asked squeezing Shaun's arm.

There were several hard battles going on around the field. Shaun searched for fox.

"Do you see 'er mate, is she okay" Trevor coughed.

(Jesus, what a man Shaun thought looking at Trevor. He fought an entire army by himself without flinching, all for the love and respect of his Fox. I will not let this man die, not for my cause; I have enough blood on my hands already).

"Tag, I need you girl" Shaun hollered.

The tiny blue-gold dragon dropped out of the sky right beside Trevor. She looked into Shaun's eyes and saw fire there. It was not a tiny flicker but an entire inferno within. She felt now was the right time.

"Shaun hear me, Malfeezanz and trash he was; told you the truth before his time was up, Ayla lives and she is in there" Tag said pointing at the keep.

"I do not think that is funny, you are not beyond my power to smite Tag" Shaun snarled in fury!

"What gain is there for me to lie to you my friend" Tag said softly?

In a clearing behind the Keep, Rolf was trying to sneak off. Open combat was not his thing. Rolf was very powerful fully transformed, but even then, come on dragons, giants, crazy humans with magic thunder. No, Rolf just wanted to get the hell out dodge, and I mean yesterday. He was not so lucky thought. A red flash went across his face. Blood began to drip from his muzzle. He howled.

"What show yourself so I can kill you" Rolf roared. He transformed completely into a Werewolf.

"For your crimes against the world I sentence you to death Rolf, you're a mangy dog that I must put down" said Fox

Rolf saw her standing in the shadow of a tree; she was truly the Goddess of the wilds he thought. Sadly, he was going to kill her, and then he would rape her dead body. He lunged at her. Fox moved so fast Rolf did not even know she had moved until her foot hit him squarely in the nuts, then he knew. Fox was not even closed to done. She stomped on his Achilles heel and tore the tendon off the bone on his left ankle. Rolf Screamed in pain.

"I believe that once Thurv warned you against me mutt, and you did not listen then, foolish as I have no equal in hand to hand combat" Fox growled.

The Werewolf was not dead yet, therefore he was still dangerous. He faked a collapse to get Fox in close to him. She did indeed come closer, and when she was in range, Rolf lunged at her. He took her down and sat on her stomach.

"Not so tough now are you little Fox pup. Where is all your big talk now? I am stronger than you, so you're dead" Rolf said all snide.

(Laughter)

"You stronger than me, absurd" Fox laughed.

Rolf was about to sink his saliva covered teeth into Fox's throat when she stood up. She grabbed him by the throat and threw him into a tree forty feet away. Before Rolf hit the ground, Fox hit him ten more times. Fox moved so fast with no sound that Rolf did not know where she was until he heard her whisper in his ear.

"Time to beat the dog" Fox giggled in Rolf's ear.

The Werewolf turned about and punched the tree he thought was Fox. She was standing beside his right arm, shaking her head at his sloppy blows. A real fighter thinks ten moves ahead to beat their opponent, this fool could not even remember who he was supposed to be hitting. Here was a poor tree getting a left hook.

"I guess you have had enough" Fox said

Once again, she was a blur. She snapped a medium size branch of a tree, ran right up in front of the wolf-man, and stopped. Fox looked into Rolf's eyes and rammed the branch though his heart. Blood dripped out his mouth and out his chest.

"Coupe de grace baby" Fox whispered in Rolf's ear, and then she tore his entire head off. "Who is afraid of the big bad wolf... no one, he's dead".

Fox found Trevor trying not to sleep, even though he was poisoned and messed up. She scolded him and made him sleep, once he was safely in her arms. Fox carried Trevor far away from the war zone, they had done their part, and the rest was up to Shaun.

Sayu was walking down to where Malfeezanz was; she believed since he was a magic user, he would be her foe. She was so focused on that, she never saw the lightning that stuck her from the shadows effectively breaking her back. She wreathed on the ground in agony as a lone figure emerged.

"Poor little witch, did you forget that your betters were upon the field this day. I have wanted to put an end to your minor magic twiddling for years. I guess now I have. Strange, I thought it would be a more enjoyable victory. I guess I was mistaken, oh my" Orrin laughed.

"You were always a back jumping coward Orrin. If you are so much my senior, why not face me, instead of attacking me from behind" Sayu said in great pain.

"You might have gotten lucky and I can't let that happen, I am much too important to...me. Besides only a fool lets himself get take from behind" Orrin snickered.

"OH is that a fact"?!

A rock the size of a bowling ball went right through Orrin's spine right between his shoulder blades. It was white hot and charged with energy, so when it got into Orrin's chest cavity, it exploded. Orrin's lungs, heart, liver and stomach were all ripped to shreds.

"Mara" Sayu hissed through her pain?

"Yes darling, I am here" Mara said.

The sorceress looked at Mara with a new admiration, then at Orrin.

"Don't worry about him, I tore up his back and lungs, so he can't utter a magic spell, like healing for instance. Would you like to finish him off or leave him for now" Mara asked?

"My love, Orrin is an Elf elder he can't be killed, only contained. I would like you to help me cast a spell of containment, it is petty but I want to imprison him myself" Sayu said.

"Fine, but first, let me do this. AHNA NATHRA UUTHAS VENTHRU" Mara said in the magic tongue.

All of Sayu's pain was gone and her back stopped bleeding. Mara lifted Sayu up and carried her over to where Orrin was flopping on the earth.

"You should learn to shut your filthy mouth wizard and take care of business. I am going to send you to the pit Orrin for a millennium. You will suffer and suffer, when you return I may be no more but I will leave you a gift of great price elf trash" Sayu hissed.

"Are you ready sister" Mara said as Orrin looked directly at her.

The Elf had never noticed this powerful mage before, how had she hid her aura from him. Sister? Orrin was angry not at Mara but at himself for gloating, when he should have just finish Sayu, now the bitch had him down and out for a thousand year of pain and misery, in the pit.

Sayu held her breath and focused for a second, and then she sang in a voice so beautiful that both Mara and Orrin both cried. A rift so black it ate the light of the sun opening in front of Orrin's body. A huge black hand with flaming red nail reached out and grabbed Orrin. A second hand reached out for Sayu, but Mara cracked it with a whip made of living lightning and the hand pulled back.

"Hello again Orrin, I have missed you. (Horrible terrifying laughter from an inhuman voice). Maybe next time, Eh Sayu" The hell voice said.

The void closed and Sayu collapsed. Mara tossed out her wings, and then she swooped up her sister and carried Sayu's near dead body back to where Tag was on the wings of an angel.

"Well done my love" Mara said to Sayu.

Argast was waiting for T'relth to come out of the Keep and fight with him. He never took his eye off the Keep. He swept for Dragon magic to make sure the Black did not slip away or attack him from the back. Argast was way too powerful for T'relth to challenge face to face; therefore, treachery was the only way Argast believed. How soon he would be proved right.

"What now old friend" Shaun said?

"T'relth must come out now, his forces are beaten, and he has lost. I will demand he hand over your wife" Argast said. "Yes, I am sorry Shaun, I knew she was alive, but if I told you when I found out, you would have killed everyone trying to get her back, Ayla included".

Shaun made an angry face but did not reply. He had known there was a secret among his allies, but never knew how big it was. He knew also that Argast was right in his judgment. That did not mean Shaun liked it at all.

There was a huge explosion behind them, and T'relth jump forth out of jet-black fire, a full sized nightmare. Tag never saw the Black coming

Because she was looking after Sayu who was dying. The black dragon ran his onyx talons down Tag's golden spine spikes, ripping off about half. Tag was severely injured but she turned on the Black golden eyes blazing. She hit the Black directly in the face with a blast of pure white light, blinding him. Tag snapped up Sayu and Mara and tossed them into the air, thus saving their lives, just as the Black recovered. Tag still had her back to T'relth when he slammed his teeth into the back of her blue neck; and he shook her until she was limp, and then dropped her. T'relth turned and faced the Red, placing his armored Black fore foot on Tag's limp form.

"One of yours Red for all of mine you killed" T'relth taunted Argast.

The Pure Flame of the Inferno shot out of the Red's mouth and hit the spot T'relth was just in, barely missing Tag. The Black, being a coward and completely unable to stop that fire with anything he knew of; jumped into the void just in time. Argast jumped, spread his wings and land in one stealthy movement beside Tag. Huge oyster tears fell from his amber eyes.

"Oh my little one, I told you to watch your back, you're my nest mate, you can not die. SHAUN" screamed Argast!

Shaun could not hear him even standing beside the RED. At that very significant moment, T'relth came from the Keep carrying Ayla and another beautiful woman in his fore-claws.

The Black saw Shaun.

Shaun burst into flames like a Phoenix and shot into the sky like a missile or a flaming arrow straight for the Black. Shaun was no longer capable of speech, he intended in killing a dragon and saving his wife.

"ROAR" T'relth belched out to stop Shaun in his tracks, blew some jets of black fire.

Shaun did not even try to avoid them, he just went through. T'relth panicked when he realize that Shaun was covered in the Pure Flame of the Inferno, and he was over match by this man.

"You can have her back if you can find her again human, good luck boy" T'relth bellowed.

A jet of black flame licked the sky, that great evil black dragon T'relth turned his back on Shaun and flew in the rift, which closed the instant he was within.

"NOOOOOOOOOOO"!!!

"AYLAAAAAAAA" SHAUN SCREAMED as he fell to the earth.

DRAGON & FIRE TALE

EPILOGUE

In the instant before Shaun hit the ground the Phoenix came out of nowhere and grabbed Shaun's limp form. Shaun just seemed to have dropped over dead when his wife was taken again, and he was so close, so damn close to saving her.

Mara was coming out of the sky with Sayu in her arms. Sera and Liri were in the air just above her dropping fast as well toward where Tag lay.

Fox came running like Mercury with Trevor in her arms still refusing to rest. So strong was Trevor's will and loyalty to his friends that he could not rest not knowing if they would live or die.

Argast for all of his incredible power could do nothing for Tag or Sayu. He cried in despair for in all his long years, Argast had never know love or taken a mate. Tag had been to be the one he chose, and she was dying in his mighty talons.

The Phoenix dropped Shaun on the ground at Mara's feet. He just laid there staring at the sky.

"Shaun Tag has the power to find anything or anyone, but she is dying man" Mara said in haste. "Sayu is done for as well, unless you help them as you helped Trevor".

At that, Shaun rolled over and got up, he walked over to Tag and put his hand on her chest. He face was grime and shaded, but he did not speak. He went over to Sayu who was still awake and alive but fading. He bent down, placed his hand on her breast, face still grime kissed her.

Nothing happened.

"Everyone get away from them, NOW" He yelled as fire came out of every pour in his body and went into the Phoenix.

Shaun backed up and away from Sayu and Tag as well confusing everyone, until, he spoke. Then Terror took over for even the Red, Argast.

"Do it, sing to them" Shaun said to the Phoenix without looking.

If there was any protest, Shaun never heard it. Argast roared so loud the heavens shook. Mara screamed and cried, all the other just cried, They knew to hear the song of a Phoenix is death, think grim reaper. The Phoenix looked at Shaun for a moment, and then flew to sit on his Bothers shoulder.

The world stopped literally. The Phoenix opened it's flaming beak and sang the most GOD blessed song in the universe, and Shaun cried his heart out, what was left.

The allies took Shaun's tears as a sign of sorrow and regret, which was not correct, not even close. The Phoenix stopped and merged into Shaun, to keep him alive. So sad was Shaun that death was very near him, and the Phoenix would not leave Shaun to the reaper's cold embrace, not for a long time to come.

All the crying stopped when Tag sat up and stretched her back and yawned. Sayu cough and then leaned up and focused on Shaun.

"I love him" Sayu said. She looked around. "I love all of you, Mara, Sera, Liri, and the rest of you".

"She was pulled through time Shaun, we will get her back. I will show you the way" Tag said with confidence.

"I will be with you always Tag, if you will still have me as your mate" Argast said softly?

The group was confused, the Phoenix sang but Tag and Sayu were not dead, they were healed completely and spared death. How could this be so?

As if he was reading their minds, the fire-man spoke the truth.

"He sang the song of life" he said and spoke no more.

All the adventurers looked around at each other and suddenly they noticed. No Mickalean, where was the leprechaun?

DRAGON & FIRE TALE

LIST OF CHARACTERS:

Malfeezanz (MAL): goblin, green-ish grey four feet, 200lbs of muscle, one red eye, one blue, leader of his horde, he is wily and clever, not give to anger. Medium magic user (mostly to serve and save himself)

Trevor (Trev): human, Irish red hair, green eyed, good humored, loyal, good with small arms, ONLY one to trust Shaun. Ex-terrorist, sniper, adventurer, ladies man, brave beyond all reason, (warriors heart: Would rather die than quit)

Shaun: American, well spring of magic, he caused it to come into the world again, Dark blond-red hair, brown eyes. Power over fire of all kinds, favorite is the Phoenix fire Or the Pure flame of the inferno

Sayu: Asian, female very powerful mystic, who gains magic when Shaun opens the rift, hard case that leans toward evil, but finds Shaun a tasty reason to be good. Also a man-eater, she made MARA and the girls harpies, then restored Mara later Mara taught her about love

Argast: The RED :fire dragon, old mean unbeatable juggernaut, huge, Shaun's friend and sometimes opponent (Shaun calls him Red Storm as nobody alive knows Argast's real name but Shaun. Dragons are armored everywhere, even their eyes, and fire is not a weapon against them. The most powerful magic wielder on the planet.

T'relth: (the black) black dragon pure evil, Sayu's ally, super powerful, Argast enemy, master of magic

Brick: 1/2 rock giant, 1/2 forest giant, blue eyes and blond hair grey skin that is indestructible, 30ft tall, 2100lbs, he is sharp eyed, unlike most giants who have poor vision, he is also

219

gentle spirited and carries joy with him, has the ability to grow plant life of all sorts.

Fox: Werefox, OMG beautiful, perfect body rust-red hair, green-grey eyes, merciless hunter-killer, Shaun's tracker, friend and sometimes lover, proud, would not admit to feeling if you killed her, (except for Trevor or Shaun)

ROLF: werewolf (the big bad wolf) be afraid, grey, yellow eyes bad breath, cruel, deadly, as a human he is hansom, if he likes you he will be generous, if not well not good, will not kill any human woman who is with his child, even after birth.

Ayla: Tiny pacific islander girl, Shaun's wife who was taken by MAL (she nearly killed him with his own knife) and later by the Black dragon T'relth, Shaun thinks her dead, She helped Kala, Kamy, and the late Kit escape from Mal

Micky :(Patrick Savage Mickalean) leprechaun: 3 foot, shifty, funny, thieving, black hair (weird for a wee people) He is not normal for one of his people either, his hidden power is a rival for a dragon's

ORRIN: immortal Dark Elf, magic power is off the hook, Shaun's guide and irritation, he is the premier mage of his kind, he strives to increase his power, he is neither good nor evil, he has no allies, he wants none

Thurv: troll, massive blue green , ill tempered, Bricks sometimes companion, Thurv respects strength and power, if he can beat you, he can eat you, that is his motto, bad breath, Shaun does not like him, the feeling is shared by many
black hair and eyes (dead eyes), also important he can screech like a bat and it work as sonar, make hiding from him nigh impossible

Prime minister Lowe: Irish, hard head good man, cares for his people, ex-terrorist, mad bomber, Trevor's friend and

sometime sparring partner

Mara; Angel, snow white wings, arcane magic powers, good mannered, loving nature, was once a human, then a harpy, she has two magic companions (sera, and Liri)

Sera: Human-angel hybrid, once a girl, then a harpy, restored by Mara, she has beautiful gossamer butter fly type wings, blue eyes brown hair, loyal to Mara in all things, minor magic healing ability

Liri: human-angel hybrid like Sera, same wings, black wave hair , pale blue eyes, shy, in love with Brick (he knows)

Kala: Amazon warrior girl, black hair, bright light blue eyes, merciless, 6'2, 180lbs of Goddess, Ayla's best friend and protector (she secretly loves Ayla and Kamy)once a sex slave to MAL, Ayla set them free

Kamy: Tiny Petite human girl 17, Blond, dark blue eyes. Very clever, scared all the time, escape artist, once a sex slave to MAL until Ayla set her free

Kitten (kit) the fourth girl who escaped Mal's prison, died of a brutal rape from the goblin, died happy as a free woman thanked Kala for carrying her to freedom, Kamy's best friend. She is the spark that will ruin Mal for good in the fires to come.

PURE FLAME OF THE INFERNO: God's divine spark, the first fire in the universe (Shaun is the first human to have control of it, only **GOD** has ever used it, too dangerous to be set free. The all Mighty is watching the world of man again; they just may be saved by one man.

Phoenix fire: comes from actual Phoenix, cannot be controlled by man, only the Phoenix itself can control it, however, if a Phoenix bonds with a man, elf, dragon etc then they can as an extension use the Phoenix fire, and nothing can withstand the onslaught.

Goblins: there are two kinds (GREY: clever, very evil, not aggressive, sly, leaders, they think, smaller of the two types) Green: big 6+ ft, ill tempered, mean, brutish, evil, semi dumb, not as big and powerful as a troll, but   dangerous to normal humans and the smaller races (gnomes, fairies, Gelflings, hobbits) red eyes are a sign that they are violent and murderous

Giants there too many types that all others stem from.

ROCK: really big 30-50ft tall, 1800-5000lbs, gray or blue eyes usually, grey indestructible skin, poor eye sight, bad temper, massive strength, usually not deep thinkers, but not dumb that would be a mistake possible fatal, able to used earth magic, find water, form rock by touch

Forest: big 30foot-ish, 1800-3000lbs, green tinted skin, sandy hair, blue or green eyes, poor eyes sight, tuned to nature & all thing green (plants, trees), can used nature or green magic to grow or control plant life, forest guardians. Not as hostile as their kin, more long thinking, and fast movers, were Rock are slow, forest giants are like jungle cats.

Arkai: golden-red fairy, old, wise, clever, fearless. The size a grown man's thumb. Member of the rare Goldburst family. Adviser to Dan Lowe

Tag: Blue-Gold dragon, pigmy size of a horse, Argast's mate, clairvoyant, wise, and psychic

SAY TUNED TO THE NEXT EXCITING BOOK IN THE SERIES. THANK YOU

ABOUT THE AUTHOR:

Shane was born Dec 21st, in Portland Oregon, to his mother Toffy Lee Wilson and Oscar Joel Wilson. He has an older sister Cookie Caroline Sinclair and a younger brother Curtis Casey Wilson.

Shane currently lives in Vancouver Washington with his Wife of over twenty years, Arlene; and he son Joston and his daughter Jessica Lee.

Shane races Quads and has won 13 over all championships. Joston has won two and Jessica has one title to her credit as well.

Shane has studied Martial arts for nearly thirty years and has a 5th degree black belt in **KAJUKENBO.**

Shane loves to entertain people with his stories; so her beautiful wife bought him a laptop and told him to put them all to paper. It is Shane's goal to write 100+ books and publish them all. At his current rate; he will reach his goal in under ten years time.

Shane offers this bit of advice:

"IF YOU THINK YOU CAN; THEN YOU ARE RIGHT. IF YOU THINK YOU CAN'T THEN YOU ARE ALSO RIGHT. THEREFORE, NEVER LET ANYTHING BEAT YOU!"

MY PERSON MANTRA IS:

I CAN'T BE BEAT; BECAUSE I WONT BE BEAT.

I MAY NOT ALWAYS WIN, BUT I NEVER LOOSE.

GOD BLESS YOU AND I LOVE YOU.

BTW: STAY TUNED FOR BOOK TWO